A Simple
Christmas
Wish

A SIMPLE Christmas WISH

MELODY CARLSON

Revell

a division of Baker Publishing Group
Grand Rapids, Michigan

© 2013 by Melody Carlson

Published by Revell
a division of Baker Publishing Group
P.O. Box 6287, Grand Rapids, MI 49516-6287
www.revellbooks.com

Printed in the United States of America

Library of Congress Cataloging-in-Publication Data
Carlson, Melody.
    A simple Christmas wish / Melody Carlson.
        pages cm
    ISBN 978-0-8007-1965-4 (cloth)
        1. Orphans—Fiction. 2. Amish—Fiction. 3. Family secrets—Fiction.
    4. Forgiveness—Fiction. 5. Christmas stories. I. Title.
PS3553.A73257S55 2013
813'.54—dc23   2013010837

13 14 15 16 17 18 19   7 6 5 4 3 2 1

1

Rachel Milligan had given up on Christmas years ago. Back when family dysfunction and personal disappointments had permanently jaded her attitude toward the holidays for good. However, for the sake of her only niece—a starry-eyed six-year-old who still believed in Santa—Rachel feigned enthusiasm for the upcoming season.

"Don't you just *love* Christmastime?" Holly said happily as the two of them lugged and tugged the man-sized evergreen into the elevator with them.

"Oh yeah," Rachel muttered as she stood the tree upright, jamming it into the corner. Then, balancing the hefty greens with one elbow, she brushed pine needles off her new Michael Kors coat, hoping pine pitch wasn't too difficult to remove from ivory cashmere.

"And both of us have our birthdays at Christmastime," Holly reminded her as she peeled off her red mitten and reached up to press the button for the forty-ninth floor. "Yours comes first, doesn't it, Aunt Rachel?"

"Uh-huh." Rachel didn't care to be reminded that she

would turn thirty-five soon. Somehow this wasn't where she'd expected to be at this stage of life—just recently some archaic labels like *spinster aunt* and *old maid* had begun to flash through her head without warning. She pushed a wayward strand of sleek chestnut hair away from Holly's eyes. "And you will turn seven on Christmas Eve," Rachel said cheerfully. "Lucky girl."

Holly ran a hand over a tree branch. "Mommy and Daddy will be so surprised when they see we already got the Christmas tree." Her brown eyes twinkled with mischief, as if she thought the two of them were pulling off a high-level heist. "Can we decorate the tree too, Aunt Rachel? And put on all the lights? Can we do it all by ourselves before Mommy and Daddy get home?"

Rachel shrugged. "I don't see why not." Although in truth she was a tad uneasy about Holly's impulsive suggestion they bring home a tree today. What if Michael and Miri felt as if Rachel had stolen some holiday tradition by doing this? However, it did seem a fair trade. After all, Michael and Miri were down in the Caribbean soaking up sunshine right now. Meanwhile Rachel had sacrificed her vacation time to remain here in Chicago with Holly, where the temps, combined with the wind-chill factor, had dipped into the low teens this week.

Besides that, how was Rachel supposed to say "no" to Holly's hopeful brown eyes and charming persuasion? It didn't help that the Christmas tree man and his big yellow dog had cheerfully greeted them every single time they'd walked past his tree stand this past week. Christmas, after all, was only three weeks away, and according to Holly, *everyone* in her first-grade class already had their Christmas trees up.

The friendly tree man had also helpfully pointed out that the selection would only diminish from here on out. Really, Rachel decided as they tugged the tree out of the elevator and down the hallway, she was doing her brother and sister-in-law a favor. Never mind that the shape of this tree, fat and full, was not what Miri would've picked out. Their usual Christmas tree was tall and thin and "elegant," reaching nearly to the ten-foot ceiling.

As Rachel fumbled to retrieve the apartment key from her pocketbook, she noticed the trail of needles from the apartment door to the elevator. Maybe she should come back out and sweep it up . . . or perhaps the maintenance man would take care of that too. It never ceased to amaze her what chores he was willing to do for the tenants in this high-rise. In the house she shared with three other roommates, you cleaned up your messes.

"Let's put the tree by the windows," Holly suggested eagerly. "That way people can see it from outside."

Rachel wasn't sure how many people would look up to the forty-ninth floor to see anything, but as she recalled, it was where Michael and Miri usually positioned their tree anyway. She carefully balanced it against a column in the spacious apartment. "So, Holly, do you know where your parents keep the Christmas decorations and the tree stand and all that kind of stuff?"

Holly's mouth twisted to one side as she thought. "Maybe in the closet, down there in the hallway," she suggested as she peeled off her coat. But, naturally, there was no such luck. Together they hunted in vain throughout the spartanly furnished apartment. Every closet and storage place was neat as a pin, with crates labeled, but no Christmas decorations or tree stand were to be found.

"I'll bet those things are being stored somewhere else in the building," Rachel told Holly. She'd heard there was storage in the basement, although she had no intention of burrowing down there.

"But the tree man said we need to give the tree some water right away," Holly reminded her. "So it doesn't dry out. Remember?"

Rachel nodded, recalling how he'd cut the bottom of the tree for them, saying it would help it to soak up water. "You're right." She went to the kitchen and took out the largest mixing bowl and filled it with water, then stood the tree in it, hoping it would do for the time being. After dealing with a large puddle, which Holly sopped up from the maple-wood floor with a thick white bath towel, Rachel decided she and Holly needed to make a quick trip to the corner store.

An hour later, they returned with a brand-new tree stand and three strings of multicolored twinkle lights. By the time it was getting dusky outside, they had the tree securely in the stand with the three strands of colorful lights garlanded around and around. Rachel knew the colorful lights would be a problem for Michael and Miri, since they normally had only white lights, but for now it was fun.

"There," Rachel proclaimed as she plugged in the lights. "How's that?"

Holly clapped her hands and danced merrily in front of the tree. "It's beautiful—beautiful—*beautiful!*"

Rachel stepped back to look, smiling at their accomplishment. "It is pretty, isn't it? Even with just the lights. I think we should leave it like this, don't you?"

"No, we need *more* decorations," her niece insisted.

"You'll have to wait for your mom and dad to get home for that." Rachel headed to the kitchen sink, where she hoped to wash the sticky tree pitch from her hands.

"Or else, we can make the decorations *ourselves*," Holly called out hopefully. "Like we did at school."

So it was that they spent the rest of Saturday evening with all of Holly's arts-and-crafts materials spread across the big glass table in the dining room. With the help of colored construction paper and pipe cleaners and glitter and stickers and all sorts of odds and ends, they managed to create some rather strange but colorful tree decorations, which they placed here and there on the bushy tree.

Although it wasn't a school night, it was getting rather late, and Rachel wanted to be a somewhat responsible aunt by enforcing Holly's bedtime. But Holly insisted they make cocoa first. "And we have to drink it sitting down on the floor by the Christmas tree," she explained.

"Is that your tradition?" Rachel asked as she nuked their cups of cocoa in the microwave.

"Tradition?" Holly frowned.

"You know, the things you do every year with your parents." Rachel removed a cup, cooling it down with a bit of milk. "Do you have cocoa together after you decorate the tree?"

Holly glumly shook her head as she reached for the cup. "Mommy and Daddy decorate the tree while I'm asleep."

Rachel nodded as they returned to the great room. That

explained why Michael and Miri's Christmas trees always looked so perfect, like something out of a decorating magazine. Rachel studied the chubby tree with its funky decorations and grinned. Well, they would just have to deal with this one when they got home.

"Let's turn off all the lights," Holly said eagerly. "Except for the tree."

They extinguished all the other lights and, with their cocoa in hand, sat on the floor in front of the glowing Christmas tree. The image of the colorful lights reflected in the floor-to-ceiling windows was really stunning. Rachel couldn't help but feel some pride in their accomplishment. As they sipped their cocoa, Holly begged Rachel to sing some Christmas songs with her.

"It's our *tradition*." Holly tried out the new word. "After decorating the tree."

"Really?" Rachel said skeptically. "You and your parents have a tradition of singing under the tree?"

"No . . . not really." Holly made a sheepish smile. "I mean you and me, Aunt Rachel. It's *our* tradition. Okay?"

Well, who could reject that? Rachel agreed to this new tradition, and Holly led them in some songs she'd learned at school, traditional tunes that Rachel could barely remember from her own childhood, but she did her best to sing along.

Eventually their cocoa was gone and they'd sung "Rudolph the Red-nosed Reindeer" twice and Rachel had managed to convince her enthusiastic niece that if Santa was watching, he'd be disappointed to see that Holly was up past her bedtime. To Rachel's relief, her slightly diabolical tactic worked. After teeth brushing and one bedtime story, Holly was tucked into bed and kissed good night.

Feeling contented and tired, Rachel returned to the great room, where she made herself comfortable on her brother's black leather Eames lounge chair. As she put her feet on the matching ottoman, she admired the product of today's creative ingenuity. Okay, the tree did look a bit messy and chaotic and it was slightly crooked in the tree stand, and Michael and Miri would probably redo most of it when they got home next week, but in the meantime she knew Holly would enjoy it. And she would too.

In Rachel's opinion, the chubby, funky tree provided a nice contrast to the crisp, clean lines of the modern apartment. Rachel loved Miri, but she sometimes wondered about her sister-in-law's addiction to such extremely stark design. Whether it was the matching pair of white vinyl chairs or the sleek aqua blue couch or the glass-topped table with its pale blue crescent-shaped bowl filled with three white marble balls, everything was always in its place, and sometimes this apartment felt a bit staged. Really, what was wrong with a little well-placed clutter? She knew, however, that this was one of the things Michael appreciated about Miri.

Rachel remembered when she and Miri had been roommates more than ten years ago, back before Rachel introduced Miri to her brother and lost a favorite roommate but gained a sister-in-law. After having escaped her previous roommate, whom Rachel had secretly nicknamed Miss Piggy, she'd greatly appreciated Miri's neat-freak habits. But studying this space now, she wondered how Michael and Miri could feel at home with these lean-lined furnishings. Did they really relax amid the shiny surfaces, bare floors, and oversized pieces of modern art? Or was this simply meant to be a showplace for Michael's clients and business associates? Rachel knew they entertained frequently.

Of course, she'd never question them on this. This was their place and they could do as they liked with it. If this were her apartment, though—and sometimes she wished she had an elegant downtown space like this—she would add some touches of warmth and color and texture and interest. Holly would probably like that better too.

Rachel didn't like to tell anyone how to live their lives, particularly her older brother, Michael. He always seemed to have all the right answers. She'd always thought of him as the solution guy. She knew she would never have survived her childhood, and even parts of her adulthood, without Michael's intervention. However, if she were to give her brother one piece of loving sisterly advice, she would suggest that he slow down his fast-paced lifestyle. Between working long hours, keeping multiple social commitments, and traveling for pleasure, he seemed to be overly busy.

When Michael studied law in college, he had planned to become a public defense attorney, but outstanding grades and some good connections had lured him into a prestigious corporate law firm following graduation. It was supposed to have been a temporary stopping place, just long enough for him to pay off his student loans and build a comfortable nest egg for him and Miri. A few years later, Holly had come along and then they'd gotten a good deal on this swanky apartment. Rachel knew that the idea of leaving his lucrative position, with all its perks, had grown less and less appealing.

Even so, Rachel worried that Holly's childhood was passing her parents by, and that someday the two of them would wake up and realize their little girl was fully grown and setting off to live a life of her own without them. Of course, it wasn't really any of Rachel's business, except that she was Holly's only aunt as well as her godmother and Michael's only living relative—at least that they were aware of. So perhaps when Michael and Miri got home on Wednesday night, she would gently broach this subject with them. For Holly's sake.

While she was on the subject, maybe she'd ask them if it was time to rethink their whole nanny situation. Nanny Vida had seemed a bit elderly when she was hired shortly after Holly was born, back when Miri decided to return to work, but according to some of the stories Holly had shared, Nanny Vida was in more need of supervision than her six-year-old charge. Besides that, since Miri had given up her career and Holly was in school, it seemed frivolous to keep the nanny. Except that Miri had grown to enjoy her freedoms. Thankfully, for Holly's sake, Nanny Vida had taken her vacation simultaneously with Michael and Miri's, which was precisely why Rachel was here now.

Still, it wasn't Rachel's place to butt into these things. What did she know about child rearing or families in the first place? Their father had abandoned them when Rachel was much younger than Holly. After that, their mom had been so busy trying to provide that they'd barely even seen her. When Rachel was about twelve, their mom had gotten sick. She'd passed away right before Rachel started high school, but Michael had gotten a tiny apartment and a part-time job, and had somehow managed to get her through school and complete his education at the same time.

To be fair, she rationalized as she tidied up the craft

materials, scrubbing Elmer's glue from the glass-topped dining table, Michael was probably just making up for what he'd missed out on earlier in his life. Maybe he deserved to have some fun, as well as the chance to see some new places. After all, Rachel had been able to travel the whole world—thanks to her job as an international flight attendant. Even that was partly due to Michael's sacrifices. So what right did she have to judge him?

Although she didn't know much about Miri's childhood and upbringing, she knew enough to understand it had been difficult, and based on a few random comments, she assumed it had been impoverished as well. Was it really Rachel's place to express an opinion on how they lived their lives now? At least they provided well for Holly. She attended an exclusive private school, had a nanny (albeit a slightly senile one) and all the toys and material things a child could want. What more could Rachel expect of them? If Michael was happy practicing corporate law, why should she care?

As for being stuck in an unfulfilling career, who was she to talk? She'd been working for the same airline for close to fifteen years now. It was a job she'd planned to stick with for only as long as it took to see a bit of the world. After that, she had planned to find Mr. Right, settle down, and start a family of her own, instead of babysitting for her niece. Not that she didn't love her adorable niece.

As she rinsed out the cocoa cups, she felt inexplicably tired and wondered why she hadn't gone to bed by now. What was the point in staying up and fretting over her brother's problems—problems that she was simply imagining and overblowing anyway?

She was reaching to turn out the kitchen lights when the wall phone rang, making her jump. She fumbled to grab the receiver before it rang again, worried it might wake up Holly—and wondering who would call this late.

"I am calling in regard to Michael and Miriam Milligan," a slightly foreign-sounding voice informed her.

At first she assumed it was a solicitor's call, perhaps someone from India, and she was about to get rid of them, but something stopped her. "What do you mean?" she asked. "Regarding what?"

"Are you a relative of Michael and Miriam Milligan?" the man asked.

"I'm Michael Milligan's sister. Rachel Milligan." In that same moment, she felt a disturbing uneasiness wash over her. She braced herself.

First he named a place she had never heard of and a word she couldn't pronounce, explaining he was the chief of police, and then he informed her that there had been a plane accident early in the evening. "I am sorry to inform you that your relatives did not survive."

"Wh-what?" Rachel felt her knees weaken. "That's impossible. Their flight to Chicago wasn't scheduled until Wednesday and—"

"This was an inter-island flight," he told her. "A small plane."

Her knees seemed to melt, giving way as she sank down to the hard floor. "What did you say? Tell me again. *Who* are you? *Where* are you calling from?"

He went through the unfamiliar names once more, but now it felt as if her head was spinning, as if her whole world was spinning. This had to be a bad dream. A very bad dream.

"But my brother and sister-in-law aren't staying in the place you mentioned," she said eagerly. "You must have the wrong people. Michael and Miri are staying at a resort in Turks and Caicos," she proclaimed. "I have the phone number right here and—"

"Yes, I'm sorry to be unclear. Mr. and Mrs. Milligan were not staying here on our island. They were passengers on a flight that goes past here. The plane was en route. The destination was Turks and Caicos. I called the hotel there and they gave me this phone number so that I could inform you of this tragedy. I am so sorry."

"But how?" she demanded. "How could this happen?" She remembered the line she'd used hundreds of times to soothe nervous passengers: *"Airline travel is safer than driving our freeways."*

"They believe the airplane experienced a mechanical problem. A cruise ship witnessed the explosion right before it went down a few miles north of Saint Eustatius. There was a search . . . and I am sorry to inform you there were no survivors."

"But that—that's impossible." She rubbed her head, trying to absorb this, knowing it couldn't be true. Michael and Miri . . . they couldn't be dead. Someone had made a mistake. A horrible, cruel mistake.

Once again, the police chief conveyed his sympathies, but then he told her to take down some phone numbers. With trembling legs, she stood up and walked to the dining room table, where she picked up a red crayon and a scrap of yellow construction paper, writing down the long numbers he was giving her. Then, after she questioned him again, he assured her that all he was saying was true.

"I am very sorry to be the bearer of such tragic news," he said finally. "If you have any more questions, please call the numbers I gave you. Again, I am so very sorry for your loss."

"Yes . . . yes . . . thank you." Her voice choked and tears began to stream down her cheeks as she eased herself into a straight-backed dining room chair. Feeling shaky and sickened, she hung up the phone and just sat there staring at it. Did that really just happen? Was it real? Or was she asleep and simply having a horrible nightmare?

She looked at the phone still in her hand and pushed the caller ID button, seeing that the strange phone number did match the one she'd written down on the yellow paper. Of course it was true. She knew she was awake. She leaned her head forward until it thumped onto the hard, cold glass of the table and allowed the tears to flow freely. She sobbed and moaned and cried, asking herself again and again—how could this happen? *Why, why, why?* It was bad enough that she should lose her only living relative—besides Holly—but for Holly to lose both of her parents all at once, well, that was just wrong—wrong—*wrong*!

2

Most people had family to call in tragic moments like this. They had mothers or fathers or siblings or aunts or grandmothers . . . but Rachel had none of these. All she had for family was Michael and Miri and Holly. And now she only had Holly. She tiptoed down the hallway to check on Holly, worried that she might've woken and overheard some of the painful conversation or Rachel's breakdown, but the sweet girl was still sleeping. Illuminated by her Dora the Explorer nightlight, she looked peaceful and serene. Poor Holly. Just like that, she had become an orphan.

Rachel went back to the great room, pacing back and forth and wringing her hands, trying to determine what she should do. She felt she needed to do *something*. Or talk to *someone*.

Finally, she decided to phone her best friend, Kayla. "I'm sorry to call so late," she began.

"Hey, it's not that late," Kayla said cheerfully. "Is it even midnight? You're still in the city, aren't you? Why don't you come down here and meet us at—"

"I need to talk to you," Rachel interrupted. "Something—

something really, really terrible has happened and I need someone to—" She was sobbing again, trying to speak but unable to make herself understood. "I'm sorry," she gasped. "It's just so awful."

"What is it?" Kayla asked with concern. "Are you all right? Should I call 9-1-1? Is Holly all right?"

"Don't call 9-1-1," Rachel told her.

"Are you still at Michael's? Do you want me to come over?"

"Can you?" Rachel asked desperately.

"Yes, of course. I'm not even that far away. I'll grab a taxi and pop over."

"Thank you." Rachel closed her phone and sank into the Eames chair, staring at the Christmas tree through her tears, which had transformed it into a wild, blurry wash of color. It looked so unreal she began to hope, once again, that this truly was a dream. However, she felt certain it was not. She closed her eyes and attempted to calm herself by taking some slow, deep breaths.

When she heard someone at the door, she leaped up and hurried to let Kayla in. Seeing her friend's concerned expression, Rachel started to cry all over again.

Kayla grabbed her and hugged her. "I'm here. It's going to be okay," she soothed.

"It's so awful," Rachel said. "I just needed someone to talk to."

"Tell me what's happened," Kayla said with her arms still around Rachel, guiding her over to the couch. "Tell me why you're so upset. I've never seen you like this." She eased her down and sat next to her. "What is it?"

The story poured out of Rachel, the words spilling out like a broken bag of marbles, and Kayla just listened with wide eyes. "Oh, my gosh! I'm so sorry," she said finally. "That's just horrible. Poor Holly. Does she know yet?"

Rachel shook her head and blew her nose. "I have no idea how I'm going to tell her."

"Well, there's no reason to wake her now."

"I guess not . . . but she'll need to know soon."

Kayla looked at the tree and sighed. "This is going to ruin her Christmas."

"Not to mention her life." Rachel pulled out another tissue. "I've got to get myself together. For Holly's sake I've got to be strong."

"Yes." Kayla gently rubbed Rachel's shoulder. "And you will. You'll be strong for her. I know you will."

"Just like Michael was strong for me when our mother died." Rachel wiped her eyes.

Kayla nodded. "That's what family does."

Rachel knew that Kayla had a big family—the kind of supportive family that rallied around whenever something big happened, whether good or bad. Rachel had no idea what that would feel like, but sometimes she'd been envious.

"So will you adopt Holly?" Kayla asked. "I assume you're all she has."

"Yes," Rachel said. "At least we'll have each other. That's something."

"You and Holly have always been so simpatico," Kayla pointed out.

"I know. We've always had this great connection. If I ever had a daughter, I'd imagine her to be just like Holly."

21

"Whenever anyone sees you two together, they always assume you're her mother."

Rachel sniffed. "Yes . . . but a mother is hard to replace."

"Even so, she's blessed to have you, Rachel. You'll be a great mother to her."

"I'm blessed to have her too." Rachel brightened ever so slightly. Despite the horrible tragedy, the idea that she would be wholly responsible for Holly was a huge comfort. She couldn't even imagine how difficult this would be if Holly had been taken from her too.

"I assume your brother had life insurance to provide for Holly."

"Yeah, I'm sure he did. Michael was always uber-responsible like that." Except for this time, she thought sadly, when he hopped on an inter-island flight in the middle of the Caribbean.

Kayla waved her hand around the room. "I assume you'll get to keep this too."

Rachel blinked. "I don't know about that. This is a pretty expensive apartment."

"But with their insurance and all, it seems like it would be a good idea to just stay put," Kayla suggested, "for Holly's sake."

Rachel considered this. "Well, it does make sense to keep her in her regular routines . . . and in her same school." She shrugged. "Hopefully, we can stay here for a while anyway. Even if we had to sell it, I'm sure it would take some time. Maybe until the end of her school year. Then we might need something more modest."

They continued talking about the practicalities of what

Rachel would do next, and eventually it all seemed to sift down into a somewhat feasible plan. By the time Kayla left— in the wee hours of the morning, since she had a flight later in the day—Rachel felt she had an actual plan to work from. On Monday she would give her notice at work. If she fully explained the situation to her supervisor, she felt certain she wouldn't be expected to return to work at all. She would also give up her room at the house she shared with the other flight attendants. Kayla already knew another employee who was looking for a place close to O'Hare. Kayla even offered to help Rachel pack up if she could wait until Kayla's day off. As Rachel finally sank into the guest room bed, she felt utterly exhausted and incredibly sad, but at least she had a plan.

"Aunt Rachel?" Holly said quietly, gently tapping Rachel's cheek with her little fingers. "Time to get out of bed, sleepyhead."

Rachel blinked and sat up. "Morning," she croaked back at her.

"Good morning, Sunshine," Holly chirped back. She had her favorite stuffed toy, a gently worn butterscotch-colored rabbit, in her arms. "Bunny and I already went out to see our Christmas tree together. The lights were still on."

Rachel shoved her feet into the pair of Uggs she'd left next to the bed. "Uh-oh. I must've forgotten to turn them off last night."

"I think we should leave them on *all* the time," Holly told her. "Day and night."

"And I think we should make some breakfast." Rachel reached for the old plaid flannel robe she'd scavenged from

Michael's castoffs many years ago. Pulling it on, she tied the belt snugly around her waist and tried not to cry as the thought of never seeing her big brother again hit her.

"Are you sad, Aunt Rachel?" Holly was studying her carefully.

Rachel forced a weak smile. "Maybe . . . a little."

"Did you have a bad dream?"

Rachel nodded. "Yes, I think I did." She swallowed against the tears threatening to spill. How was she supposed to do this—how was she supposed to break this horrible news?

Holly put her arms around Rachel's waist, hugging her. "It'll be all right."

Rachel knelt down and hugged her niece back. "Thanks, honey. I needed that."

"I know what we should do," Holly said as she led Rachel by the hand into the kitchen. "We should have blueberry pancakes for breakfast. Okay?"

"Sure." Rachel went directly for the espresso maker, routinely going through the steps while Holly chattered away at her about how she only got to have pancakes when Rachel was there and how she sometimes liked them with blueberries, but sometimes she didn't. How was it possible for a small child to have so much to say? Still, it was cheerful and much better than silence. She tried to form the words in her head, but every sentence sounded even worse than the one before. How did one tell a child her parents were dead?

Before long, they were seated at the breakfast bar with their pancakes, minus the blueberries, and eating companionably together. For a brief spell, Rachel blocked out the elephant in the room. As she sipped her espresso, she realized it wouldn't be too hard to get used to this—the idea of quitting her job

24

in order to play the parent to this loquacious child, giving up her shared house to live in a swanky city apartment that overlooked the river . . . it was all rather appealing. That is until the harsh reality hit her all over again. The ache she felt, knowing how she'd arrived at this place, seemed to choke out all sense of pleasure. How was she going to tell Holly?

"Is it Sunday today?" Holly asked as they carried their dishes to the kitchen sink.

"Uh-huh."

"Will we go to church?"

Rachel paused to look down at Holly. She hadn't really planned to go to church, but all things considered, it was probably a good idea. Maybe she would find the strength and the answers there. If nothing else, it would postpone the inevitable. "Yes. We will definitely go to church."

"We don't always go to church," Holly pointed out. "But sometimes we do."

"Well, I think we *need* to go today." Rachel looked at the clock in the kitchen, a sleek glass piece with no numbers, but still she could tell it was about nine-thirty, which meant they had about an hour. "We'll need to hurry to get ready, and I still need a shower."

She helped Holly find an appropriate outfit, laying it all out on her bed, then hurried to shower and dress herself. Yes, the idea of going to church today was suddenly very appealing. She sometimes felt guilty for all the times she'd missed church because of her erratic work schedule, but at the same time, she'd always believed that God understood such things. However, as she was getting dressed, she questioned herself. How well did she understand God? Why would he allow the plane carrying Michael and Miri to go down like that? How was she supposed to understand and accept that? How would Holly?

At just a little before eleven o'clock, Rachel and Holly were walking into the frosty churchyard. This was the same church that Rachel and Michael and their mother had attended so many years ago. The same church where they'd attended their mother's funeral, and where Michael and Miri had said their wedding vows, and now it would be the location for yet another memorial service. Rachel walked Holly downstairs to where the children's classes were held, then hurried back up in time for the beginning of the service. Glancing around the sanctuary, she could see that little had changed in here, but because she came so seldom, the faces seemed less familiar. And yet, as she slid into the pew, she felt strangely at home.

As the organist played an old hymn, Rachel remembered when she was a girl how her mother would sometimes slip her arm around her, snuggling her up close. Whether it was her imagination or not, Rachel felt a surprising sense of warmth just now—almost as if her mother were trying to comfort her, as if she understood. As if, in a way, she were here.

Rachel had slipped a small bundle of tissues into her purse, and as the old pastor, Reverend Hanson, began his sermon, talking about finding precious treasures in unexpected places, she allowed her tears to start flowing freely again. She didn't even care if others in the congregation could hear or see her. Really, if you couldn't cry in church, where could you cry?

After the service ended, a couple of older women came over to speak to her. They seemed vaguely familiar, but she didn't recall exactly who they were. They reintroduced themselves as

Viola and Mabel. They claimed they remembered her mother and how sad it was when she passed. Hearing this, Rachel decided to open up, telling them of this most recent tragedy.

"Oh, you poor baby." Viola wrapped her big brown arms around her in a warm bear hug. "You poor, poor dear."

"And my niece is downstairs right now," Rachel sobbed. "I haven't even told her yet."

Now both of the women hugged her, holding her between them like two mother hens. Then they ushered her directly to Reverend Hanson, who was standing in the back. Viola quickly explained Rachel's situation to him, and he too hugged Rachel, expressing sympathy, then prayed for her and for Holly.

"Thank you." She wiped her eyes with the last of her wad of tissues. "Thank you all." She gave them a shaky smile. "I really appreciate your support. I needed that."

"And you'll call me to schedule the memorial service tomorrow morning?" Reverend Hanson reminded her. "I'm not positive, but I believe the church is available on Thursday morning. If you think that's okay, I can pencil it in."

"That's probably fine, but I will call you."

"We'll arrange with the women to have meals delivered to you and Holly for the next two weeks."

"Oh, that's not necessary."

"You must allow us do this," Mabel insisted. "It'll be one less thing for you to concern yourself with."

"And we'll organize a lunch to follow the memorial service on Thursday," Viola said.

"But I—"

"Don't argue with your elders." Mabel shook a friendly

finger at her. "You don't have your mother around to help you out, so why not let us?"

Rachel nodded, thanking them again. "I better go get Holly before she starts getting worried."

"We'll be praying for you, dear," Viola assured her as they accompanied her to the stairs. "For both you and little Holly."

"Yes." Mabel nodded so eagerly her chins shook. "We will pray that God gives you just the right words for the child."

"Are there any right words?" Rachel asked them.

Viola held up her hands. "I don't know about that, but I do believe love speaks louder than words. And it's plain to see you've got plenty of that."

Fortunately, Holly wasn't the last child in the classroom. She seemed intent on finishing up the nativity scene she was coloring, so Rachel didn't even bother to rush her. Instead she wandered around the room, remembering how she had attended Sunday school in this same room three decades ago. Like the rest of the church, not much had changed here either. Even though it seemed a little faded and dowdy, it was comforting. Rachel had almost forgotten those days. But, as Holly's godmother and now her guardian, she would see to it that Holly grew up getting all the spiritual training necessary to ensure a happy and healthy life.

Holly chatted cheerfully and obliviously as they rode the train back into the city. The whole while, Rachel felt distracted as she tried to formulate a plan for telling Holly about her parents' deaths. She knew this was not going to be easy. She couldn't keep putting it off, but then instead of going directly to the apartment, Rachel decided to stop at one of the nearby restaurants for some lunch. That way

Holly would have something in her stomach before hearing the bad news.

They both ordered tomato basil soup and grilled cheese sandwiches, then quietly ate, dipping corners of their sandwiches into the soup.

"We like the same things, don't we?" Holly said as they were finishing up.

Rachel nodded. "Yes, we do."

"Do we both like ice cream for dessert?" Holly asked hopefully.

Rachel smiled. "I suppose we do."

The inevitable was postponed for a while longer as they indulged in ice cream. Eventually they were back inside the apartment, and after they'd both changed into comfortable clothes, Rachel invited Holly to join her under the tree. This time, she gathered some pillows and blankets to make a more comfortable place.

"I have something really, really hard to tell you," Rachel began. "It's something that's really, really sad."

"What's wrong?" Holly frowned. "Are you going away, Aunt Rachel?"

"No, no, I'm not going anywhere."

Holly looked relieved. "Oh."

"But it's still very, very sad news, and I know you're going to be quite upset. I was really upset when I heard it. I didn't understand it. To be honest, I still don't understand it, and I'm still very, very sad."

Holly's face looked so intent that she seemed close to tears, and Rachel knew she needed to just get it out.

"It's about your mommy and daddy," she said slowly. "Last

night I got a phone call from where they're at—you know, on their vacation trip."

"In the Caribbean?" She said *Caribbean* slowly, as if she was dissecting it into small pieces.

"Yes, that's right. The Caribbean."

"For their anniversary," Holly added in a mature-sounding voice.

"Yes, that's right too. I almost forgot it was to celebrate their anniversary—their tenth." Rachel swallowed hard against the lump building in her throat. "As I was saying, I got a phone call last night and was told that your mommy and daddy were on a small airplane, flying from one island to another. There was a problem. The plane didn't make it to the island. It crashed into the ocean."

Holly's brown eyes grew larger. "It crashed?"

Rachel nodded. "Your mommy and daddy died in the crash, Holly." She waited for Holly to absorb this.

"Mommy and Daddy?" Holly's chin quivered.

"They died in the crash." Rachel was crying now. "And they can never come back home to us, Holly. They are with God in heaven now."

Holly's eyes filled with tears, and they began pouring down her cheeks as Rachel took her into her arms, gently rocking her as they sat at the foot of the Christmas tree. "That's why I was so sad this morning," Rachel explained. "I didn't really know how to tell you. Your daddy and mommy were my only family too. Well, except for you. And now all we have is each other, Holly. You and me."

Holly pulled back and looked into Rachel's face with tear-filled eyes. "Are you going to live with me and take care of me?"

"Yes," Rachel said. "It's just you and me now. We have to take care of each other. Do you think we can do that?"

Holly nodded. "Uh-huh."

Rachel hugged her again and together they cried some more, holding on to each other and rocking back and forth, letting their tears flow freely. After a while, they both lay down on the pillows and blankets beneath the tree and looked up at it, talking about Michael and Miri, taking turns sharing their favorite memories. Rachel told Holly about how excited her parents were when she was born. She told her stories about her parents that Holly had never heard before or had been too little to remember. They stayed under the Christmas tree for a couple of hours, having their own private memorial service, talking and weeping and remembering, until eventually, Holly fell asleep. Not wanting Holly to wake up all alone, Rachel remained there with her . . . thinking and praying and hoping that they were both going to be okay.

3

Rachel decided that the best way for Holly to get over the shock and sadness of losing her parents was to go back to school and resume her normal routine as soon as possible. On Monday, instead of just dropping Holly off at the front door, Rachel went into school with her, getting there early enough to speak to the principal and her teacher, informing them of the situation. Naturally, they wanted to do all they could to help Holly make the necessary adjustments. They promised to call Rachel if any problems developed. Rachel bent down to kiss Holly, who was acting surprisingly brave, and it was only as Rachel walked out of the building that she realized she would probably miss Holly more than Holly would miss her.

Still, Rachel had plenty to do to keep herself busy, and as soon as she got home, she made a detailed to-do list—everything from giving notice on her job, to making arrangements in the Caribbean, to contacting Michael's law firm, to preparing announcements for the newspapers, to reserving the church, to letting Nanny Vida know. The list grew as she remembered more things that needed doing. Some she was able to check off, and before she knew it, it was time to go pick up Holly.

So the week went, with Rachel putting most of her energy into caring for Holly and keeping her life on track by helping her make sugar cookies to take to school and attending the school's Christmas program, as well as packing up and moving her own things into the apartment, and attending to all the various details surrounding the deaths of Michael and Miri. There was hardly a moment to spare, and Rachel was very thankful for the regular delivery of dinners from the church ladies.

By Thursday, Rachel was relieved that it was the day of the memorial service. Not because she was looking forward to it, but simply because she was longing to move on, to create some sense of normalcy. The service was surprisingly well attended and went relatively smoothly. Both Rachel and Holly had cried so much during the past week that they were somewhat dry-eyed by Thursday, until the photos Rachel had put on a CD were shown up on the big screen—with some of Miri and Michael's favorite songs playing along. The combination brought most everyone to tears.

When the service and luncheon came to an end, Rachel and Holly went home to the apartment, where Rachel finally felt like she could just relax after having survived one of the longest weeks of her life. Fortunately, Holly was officially on Christmas break now, and they could both just kick back, comfort each other, and do as they pleased until mid-January. Friday, the day after the memorial service, Rachel proclaimed Pajama Day, and they didn't even get dressed. Instead they lazed around, watched Disney movies, and ate popcorn and ice cream, but at least they had a nutritious dinner when one of the church ladies dropped off a chicken-and-broccoli casserole.

"I want another Pajama Day," Holly announced on Saturday morning. Rachel was glad to agree. After all, they were on vacation. However, she insisted they should eat a bit more healthily this time. "And tomorrow we have to get up, get dressed, and go to church," she reminded her.

During the following week, Rachel added more structure to their lives by planning one Christmas-related event for each day. On Monday, they went to the Museum of Science and Industry to see the Christmas Around the World display. On Tuesday, they went to Navy Pier for the Winter Wonderfest. On Wednesday, they went to the Lincoln Park Zoo to see Santa's Safari and the ice carving demonstrations. On Thursday, they waited until dusk and went to the Brookfield Zoo to enjoy the million lights, the laser show, and all the other festivities.

On Friday morning, however, just as they were preparing to set out for a Christmas window-shopping tour along the Magnificent Mile, Walt Swanson called. Walt had been Michael's boss and mentor and Rachel had already had a conversation with him regarding her responsibilities with Holly, but he'd told her they would meet to go over the legal details of Michael and Miri's will and estate later. It seemed that later had come.

"I hope you've had enough time . . . you know, to rest and recover . . . especially after all you and Holly have been through." He spoke haltingly, almost as if something was troubling him. "But I think it's time to go over some things now. Can you come by my office this afternoon, around two?"

The law office was on Michigan Avenue, not far from the apartment, and so after their window-shopping trip and a lunch of hot dogs from a street vendor, they set out for Swanson, Myers, and Milligan.

"Your daddy always loved walking to work," Rachel told Holly as she held her hand to cross the street. It felt so natural talking to Holly like this. They had both gotten comfortable talking about things Michael and Miri *used* to do—what they liked and what they didn't. Rachel felt that speaking openly like this somehow helped to keep them alive, and that seemed important—at least for now. Perhaps the time would come when a whole day would pass and neither of them would mention the dearly departed, but Rachel doubted it would be anytime soon.

"You can wait in here," Rachel told Holly as they walked into the law office.

"I know." Holly nodded importantly. "I've waited in here before. Lots of times. Sometimes when I came with Daddy. Sometimes when Mommy brought me." She pointed to the door that still had Michael's name on it. "That's Daddy's office right there. Sometimes I went inside to see him. Sometimes I waited out here while Mommy went in to see him."

Walt Swanson came out of his office. He gave Holly a sad little smile, grasping her hand in his big one. "How is my favorite little lady?"

She smiled back. "I'm fine, thank you. How are you?"

He grinned. "I'm doing all right." He nodded to the reception desk. "I think Donna's got some Christmas candy over there." He glanced at Rachel. "If that's okay?"

"A little won't hurt," Rachel told him, looking at Holly. "Just don't overdo it. Remember we're trying to cut back on sweets."

Holly went over to Donna's desk while Walt led Rachel into his office. Although she'd been in Michael's office many times, she'd never been in Walt's. Since Walt was the boss, his office was naturally bigger and more impressive than Michael's.

"Have a seat." Walt waved to a pair of leather chairs.

She sat down and waited, curious as to why this face-to-face meeting was necessary. Perhaps there was more paperwork, or something she needed to sign in person.

Walt cleared his throat. "As you know, Michael was like a son to me. I cannot even tell you how sad I am to lose him."

She nodded. "We all are."

"Yes . . . I know."

"But at least I have Holly." She sighed. "That makes all the difference."

"Ah yes—that is precisely what we need to talk about today."

Something about his tone—or was it his words?—felt like an alarm going off inside of her. "What do you mean?" She studied him closely, watching as he folded his hands, then unfolded them.

"There's no easy way to say this, Rachel. I would've told you last week, except that I knew your hands were full. Plus I knew you were still in the midst of your grief. I had hoped . . . I had really hoped . . . there would be another way out of this."

"Out of what?" Her mouth felt dry.

"I know how much you love Holly, Rachel. I know that you expected to have full custody of her."

"Of course," Rachel said quickly. "Why wouldn't I?"

He grimaced. "Because of Michael and Miriam's will."

"What do you mean?"

He pulled a folder to the center of his desk. "At my encouragement, Michael made a new will right after Holly was born."

"Certainly. That makes sense. I assume everything has been left to Holly. Probably to be held in trust until she's of—"

"Yes, yes, that's true, but that's not the problem." He drummed his fingers on the top of the folder. "If there was any legal way to change this, I would do so, Rachel."

"Change what?"

"The guardianship of Holly has been awarded to someone else."

Rachel felt as if she'd been punched in the stomach. "What?"

"As I recall you were out of the picture when Holly was born."

Rachel took in a fast breath to remember that dark era of her life—the only time when she and Michael had been at odds, and all because of Curtis Garmin. "Well, yes . . . I suppose I was sort of out of the picture, in a way."

"I was honestly quite surprised that Michael hadn't changed their will in the past several years," Walt continued. "My assistant and I actually searched everywhere just in case there was a copy of a more recent will. These things do happen, however—especially to younger people. You never think you're really going to die, and certainly not a couple dying together."

"I'm still confused." Rachel could hear the tremor in her voice. "Who would they possibly give Holly to? To you?"

Walt frowned. "I wish they had granted custody to me, Rachel. In that case, you and I could easily work this out."

"Who, then?"

"To Miriam's sister."

"Miri has a sister?" Rachel was shocked. "Are you certain?" He nodded grimly.

"But she never spoke of her. Never spoke of any family."

"Because she was estranged."

"But if she was estranged from her family—why would she give her only child to one of them?"

"Apparently Miriam trusted her sister to properly care for Holly."

"But Holly doesn't even know this woman. Who is she? Where does she live?" Rachel stood now, pacing back and forth. "For all we know, Miri's sister could be some sort of lowlife—a drug addict or a prostitute or a murderer. From what little I knew of Miri's family, there was something really bad and wrong—something that Miri had run away from—something she never wanted to speak about. She buried it deep." Rachel stopped pacing and looked helplessly at Walt. "We can't just hand Holly over to criminals, can we?"

He made an uneasy smile. "They're not criminals."

"How do you know?"

"Because I've been in contact with the sister. Her name is Lydia Miller. And she's got several children already."

"If she has several children, why does she need Holly?" Rachel demanded.

"I'm not sure she needs Holly, but according to the law, she will be awarded custody of Holly. The will is watertight."

"What if Holly doesn't want to go? Where does this Lydia live anyway? Will Holly have to quit her school to move there?"

"Lydia lives in Ohio. Holmes County."

"Ohio?"

"In an Amish settlement."

"Amish?" Rachel suddenly imagined women in bonnets and horse-drawn carriages, but these images didn't make sense. "Miri's family is Amish?"

"Miriam grew up Amish," Walt explained. "To be honest, I was as surprised as you are. Miri always struck me as a very modern sort of girl. I never would've guessed she was Amish."

Now Rachel was remembering some things from when she'd first met Miri. Just little things, but they did seem to make sense. In a crazy, backward sort of way. She sat back down and let out a long sigh, peering hopelessly at Walt. "You're really going to take her away from me?"

"I don't want to do this, Rachel—you know I don't—and it's hard not being angry at Michael for not planning better."

"Do you think there's another will somewhere?" she asked. "In his house, perhaps?"

"It's a possibility. Do you have access to his safe?"

"No. I didn't even know he had a safe."

"Oh, sure, he's got a safe. An apartment like that? I'm certain of it. Look behind some pictures or in the back of his closet. You'll find it."

"How would I get into it?"

"You'd call in an expert. Donna can give you a reliable phone number."

"Well, that's it, then." She stood. "There has to be a safe. And in it, we'll find a more recently written will. Maybe he wrote it out just before this last trip."

Walt looked hopeful. "That's possible, but I would've expected him to leave a copy with me. I have copies of everything else pertaining to his estate."

"Maybe he was in a hurry."

Walt reached out to shake her hand. "I hope you're right, Rachel."

"I'm sure of it."

"But if you're wrong—if there is no second will—Holly needs to be delivered to her aunt in Ohio within the week."

"Within the week?"

"That's what Lydia told me."

"You spoke to her?"

He nodded.

"I thought the Amish didn't have phones or electricity. How did you speak to her? Did you go out there?"

"I sent her a telegram and she called me from someone else's phone. We spoke at length. If it's any comfort, she seems like a good person, and she really loved Miriam. She was quite shocked and saddened to hear of her baby sister's death. She was very glad to hear that Holly is coming to live with her, and she told me they live on a farm with cows and pigs and chickens and all sorts of things. She felt it was best to get Holly settled in during winter break. That way she can start back to school in January with the other children."

"They have a school?"

41

"Sure. Why wouldn't they?"

"I don't know. I guess I really don't know much about the Amish. I thought maybe they homeschooled or something."

"Well, Lydia mentioned a school. And, anyway, if you don't find a more recent will, you can be assured that Holly will be in very good hands." He made a stiff-looking smile. "And that will allow you to get on with your life, Rachel. I know you're a flight attendant. Not exactly an easy career for a guardian of a young child, being on the go all the time like that."

"I quit my job," she said in a flat tone.

"Oh, well, I'm sure they'd happily take you back."

She sighed. Maybe they would happily take her back. But would she happily go? "Anyway, I intend to find Michael's new will. I'll get back to you as soon as I do."

"Good luck."

Rachel kept the emotions from her face and her voice as she and Holly walked back home. As soon as they were in the apartment, her search for the safe began. "What are you looking for?" Holly asked curiously.

"Your daddy had a safe. I need to find it."

Holly's brow creased. "What's a safe?"

"A place where you keep important or valuable things. Sometimes it's behind a picture on a wall."

"Oh, you mean the little box inside the wall?"

"Yes," Rachel said eagerly.

Holly led her to a modern-art painting in the master bedroom that covered "the little box inside the wall." Rachel peered down at Holly. "You don't happen to know the combination, do you?"

Holly looked confused. "Huh?"

Rachel laughed. "No, of course not." She called the number that Donna had given her, and after a few hours, a man came and deftly opened it. After she paid him for his services, she carefully removed the contents of the safe, only to find a nice stash of cash, some of Miri's jewelry, their marriage license, and a few other pieces. No will.

"Did you find what you wanted?" Holly asked from where she was sitting on the bed.

Setting the contents back into the safe, Rachel just shook her head. She closed the door and replaced the painting. "No, I didn't." She sat down next to Holly and thought hard. "Is there any other place Michael kept things?" she wondered out loud.

"Mommy and Daddy keep things in their closet," Holly told her. "And in drawers." So they carefully went through every possible space until Rachel was convinced she knew every square inch of the apartment by heart.

"What about storage in the basement?"

Holly just shrugged.

Rachel called down to maintenance, and the guy in charge explained which unit belonged to their apartment. "You'll need a key to unlock it. The tenants provide their own padlocks." She thanked him, and remembering where she'd seen some miscellaneous keys, she returned to find one that was marked for the storage unit. Naturally, Holly wanted to go down with her. On their way down, Holly pointed out her dad's car, still parked in its spot in the garage. Rachel stared longingly at the old red Volkswagen Karmann Ghia, remembering how Michael had taught her to drive in that car—back before it was so beautifully restored. They continued on down to the storage area and found the right unit. The key worked, but after a long search Rachel knew that no legal documents would be stored down here. They did find the Christmas decorations, however, as well as a couple of boxes of wrapped Christmas presents, which Holly insisted on lugging back to the apartment and arranging beneath the tree.

After the gifts were placed under the tree, Holly looked up at Rachel, asking her again if she'd found what she was looking for.

Rachel just shook her head. "No, and that means you and I need to talk."

Holly blinked. "Did I do something bad?"

"No, no. Not at all. It's not that kind of talk." She took Holly's hand. "But this talk might require some ice cream. I think we still have a carton of rocky road in the freezer." As she led the way to the kitchen, she silently asked God to help her with what was sure to be another difficult conversation.

4

They were seated across from each other at the breakfast bar, quietly eating their ice cream while Rachel tried to think of a way to begin. "You know when we went to see Walt this afternoon?"

"Uh-huh." Holly nodded as a streak of brown ice cream ran down her chin.

Rachel slid a napkin over to her, pointing at her chin. "Well, Walt had some, uh, some interesting news for us."

"What news?" Holly took another bite.

Rachel knew she needed to put a positive spin on this. She needed, for Holly's sake, to act like this was all wonderful news. "For starters—you, my dear, have another aunt."

Holly looked up with wide eyes. "I have another aunt? You mean besides you?"

Rachel tried to keep her face pleasant as she nodded. "Yes. I was quite surprised too. It seems your mommy has a sister."

"My mommy has a sister?" She tipped her head to one side as if trying to grasp this. "I always wished I had a sister."

"Well, you might get your wish." Rachel couldn't remember

if Walt had mentioned whether Lydia's other children were boys or girls, but as she recalled he'd said there were several. "Anyway, you'll either have brothers or sisters or both."

Holly looked stunned. "I have *brothers and sisters*?"

Rachel caught her mistake. "I'm sorry. Actually, they're *cousins*."

"I have cousins?" Holly brightened. "My friend Allison has lots and lots of cousins. She's always telling me about her cousins. Now I have cousins too?"

Rachel smiled. "Yes, you do."

"Can I play with them?"

"Yes," she said. "In fact, you will be seeing them soon. Even before Christmas." They'd been using the advent calendar to count the days until Christmas, so she knew Holly could easily grasp this time concept.

"Are they coming here to see me?" Holly's eyes lit up. "For my birthday?"

"No. Actually, you will be going to visit them."

"Really? Where do they live?"

"Someplace in Ohio. It's called Holmes County."

Holly gave her a blank look.

"Walt told me your aunt and cousins live on a farm."

"On a farm?" she said enthusiastically. "I've always wanted to go visit a farm!"

"Great. I hear they have cows and pigs and all sorts of things."

"And horses too?" she said ecstatically. "Do they have horses, Aunt Rachel? I've always dreamed of riding a real live horse."

The image of the old-fashioned people in the horse-drawn

carriages came to her again. "Yes, I'm sure they have horses too, Holly."

Now Holly was so deliriously happy she completely forgot about the rest of her ice cream. Instead, she was dancing around the room, singing about horses and farms and Christmas. It was so good to see her happy like this that Rachel knew she had to play along. She had to act as if there was nothing better than going to see this Aunt Lydia and the cousins and the farm. If Holly assumed it was only a visit, what did it really matter? They could sort out the rest of the details later.

And perhaps, if Rachel got lucky, she might be able to explain the whole situation to Lydia. She could plead her case and beg Miri's older sister to let Holly remain in Rachel's care. Maybe she could even offer Lydia something in exchange. Rachel didn't have much in her savings, but she would gladly use all of it if she could just keep Holly with her. Not a bribe exactly—but a gift perhaps.

As she rinsed the ice cream dishes, she began to feel a smidgeon of hope again. It was possible that Aunt Lydia didn't really want any more children underfoot. And perhaps she would be a kind, generous person who would understand how much Rachel needed her only niece—especially after losing her only brother. Really, it seemed entirely possible. After all, it was Christmastime, and she and Holly had already been through so much. Maybe miracles still happened. With all this in mind, she phoned Walt and got the necessary information for Lydia Miller, explaining how she planned to drive to Holmes County and convince the mystery aunt that Holly belonged with her, right here in Chicago.

"We'll leave first thing in the morning," she informed him. "I'll use Michael's car."

He wished her luck, and after she hung up, she announced the good news to Holly.

"You know how to drive Daddy's car?" Holly asked in surprise.

"Sure. I learned how to drive in your daddy's car."

"Mommy doesn't drive," Holly said somberly. She still sometimes talked about her parents as if they were still alive. Rachel wouldn't correct her.

"I know." Rachel considered how Miri had never wanted to learn to drive. Maybe this had something to do with her Amish roots.

"Mommy hated riding in cars," Holly continued.

"But she liked the train," Rachel reminded her. "And flying in airplanes."

Holly frowned. "But their airplane crashed."

Rachel nodded. "I know. So, anyway, if tomorrow's weather is sunny like today, we should have a very nice drive through the countryside. And before you know it, you'll be seeing your aunt and your cousins and the horses on the farm." Fortunately, these expectations vanquished the gloom from Holly's face, and she was soon doing her happy dance around the room again.

"We'll pack our bags tonight," Rachel explained. "That way we can get an early start."

"What should I pack?" Holly asked.

Rachel considered this. In the unlikely event that Lydia turned her down, it would be best if Holly had whatever she needed with her. However, she couldn't bear to think that would actually happen. "Just pack whatever you like," she told her. "Anything you think you'll need if we stay for a while."

"How long will we be there?" Holly asked as she set some of her favorite toys on her bed.

Rachel shrugged. "I don't know. We'll see. Just keep in mind, your daddy's car is kind of small. You can't pack too much." She selected a few bags and set them in Holly's room. "Let's stick with these."

To Rachel's relief, the sky was sunny and clear as they headed out the following morning. Michael's 1967 fire-engine red Karmann Ghia started up on the first try. Although Rachel didn't drive much, it all came back to her as she put the car into gear. The car seemed to be in good shape, but then Michael had spent many years and lots of dollars having it completely restored. Miri had wanted him to get rid of it after Holly was born, claiming it wasn't suitable for a family, but since he had unlimited access to a company car, he insisted they hold on to this classic. It was his "baby."

With every space of the compact convertible filled with Holly's toys, clothes, and their Christmas presents, which Holly had insisted they bring in case they stayed until Christmas, there was just enough room for Rachel's one small overnight bag. She hoped that was all she would need. The more Rachel considered the whole situation, the more confident she felt that Lydia was going to see her side and agree to let Holly return to Chicago after spending a day or two in the country. They would bring their Christmas presents back to the apartment, and after celebrating Holly's birthday on Christmas Eve, they would open them on Christmas morning, using that time to remember Michael and Miri—and looking forward to their future together.

"What a perfect day for a drive," she told Holly after she'd topped off the gas tank and was heading out onto the freeway. "Nothing but sunshine for as far as I can see."

"Can we take the top down?"

Rachel laughed. "It's not *that* nice. The wind would freeze us into ice cubes."

"Oh, that wouldn't be good." Holly grinned up at her. Because there were no rear seat belts, she was seated in the passenger seat in front. Not ideal, but at least it would afford her a good view of the countryside once they got out of town.

"Daddy used to take the top down when it was warm outside," Holly told her.

"Did you go in the car with him a lot?" Rachel asked.

"Uh-huh. Mommy never went. But I did. I was never scared to ride in the car."

Rachel smiled. "I'll bet you and your daddy had some fun rides."

"Yeah. We did."

The car got quiet, so Rachel turned on the radio to a station playing cheerful Christmas songs, and the two of them attempted to sing along. Before long, the gloom seemed to evaporate. Wasn't this just what they needed, Rachel thought as the city faded away behind them—a road trip to forget all their troubles?

Oh, she was fully aware she could be driving straight into

even more troubles, but she didn't think so. For some reason she expected Miri's older sister to be a reasonable woman. Why else would Miri have granted her custody of her only child?

Of course, this only reminded Rachel of why she hadn't been listed in that important section of Michael and Miri's will. And a painful reminder it was—something she usually tried to block out of her mind. Now, however, as they drove and Holly attempted to sing along to "Frosty the Snowman," it all came rushing back at her.

About nine years ago, Curtis Garmin had stepped into her life in a big and flamboyant way. By then she'd been working for the airline long enough to know that pilots were risky at best, but something about this tall, handsome guy—his sparkling blue eyes and sandy brown curls—had pulled her right in.

Unfortunately, she wasn't the only flight attendant who'd gotten pulled in by his charming good looks, but as far as she could see, she was the only one who'd caught his eye. Perhaps that was only because she'd been holding him at arm's length, an attempt to respect the airline's no-dating-coworkers policy, even though she knew her fellow workers usually ignored it, secretly dating pilots as they liked. As a result of Rachel's prim resistance, Curtis had seemed to pursue her with more determination.

Although recently married, Miri had still been working for the airline when Rachel and Curtis first started dating. In the beginning, Miri seemed to approve of Curtis. She even talked about the possibility of another wedding in the family, but something seemed to change in the next year as Curtis and

Rachel continued their relationship. Suddenly Miri began making claims that Curtis was untrustworthy and no-good, saying that Rachel should break up with him. Rachel simply attributed her sister-in-law's paranoia to Miri's somewhat unwanted and unexpected pregnancy. Naturally, when Rachel suggested this, it only irked Miri more, and she insisted Michael should intervene on Rachel's behalf. Michael, playing the part of overprotective big brother and caring husband, tried to straighten Rachel out. Unfortunately, that only made things worse.

Shortly before Holly's birth, Rachel was not speaking to either Michael or Miri, and they seemed to have written her off completely. They didn't even invite her to join them for the holidays. She had decided if she had to choose between the man she loved and her judgmental family, she would go with the man she loved. After all, Michael had Miri now, and they were soon to have a baby. What did they need of her? As a result, she completely missed the birth of her niece, as well as some other memorable moments during Holly's first year of life.

Just thinking of this now made her unbearably sad. If she'd just known how limited her time with Michael and Miri would be—and now perhaps even losing Holly—she would've handled things differently. It was shortly before Holly's first birthday that Rachel had begun to see the signs, furtive glances exchanged between Curtis and other flight attendants followed by some unbelievable explanations. She knew it was the proverbial writing on the wall. Yet it wasn't until she found Curtis in a very compromising position with one of her roommates that it all hit the fan.

It still burned to realize she'd ignored her only niece for almost a year—all for a selfish, deceitful man who had ultimately broken her heart. The memory of having to confess to Miri and Michael that they were absolutely right about Curtis being a complete jerk still humbled her. At least they had welcomed her back into their tiny fold with open arms. They'd even asked her to be Holly's godmother, which they celebrated on Holly's first birthday. And they very graciously never spoke Curtis's name around her again. They never said, "We told you so." It was because of that unfortunate relationship, however, that she'd been written out of the will. It felt like adding insult to injury to realize that Michael had never remembered to change that important detail in their will. She hoped it was not too late.

5

The good weather continued until after they'd stopped for lunch in Angola. As they were leaving Indiana, it became obvious, by the thick bank of gray clouds gathering in the east, that the weather was changing. Rachel hadn't really considered the possibility of severe winter weather, and she knew this Karmann Ghia wouldn't be the most reliable vehicle if they ran into serious snow. In a worst-case scenario, she could use some of her free air miles to allow them to fly back to O'Hare if they got snowed in during their visit to Holmes County.

With Bunny in her arms, Holly drifted off to sleep as the car pressed on into Ohio. Rachel turned off the radio and decided to just enjoy the quiet sound of the wheels on the road, taking in the scenery around her. She'd printed out directions from the computer, and after an hour in Ohio, she found herself on a lovely country road.

"Are we almost there?" Holly blurted out as she sat up straight in her seat.

"We're definitely getting closer." Rachel pointed out the window. "Look at this pretty countryside."

To entertain themselves, they played the I-spy-with-my-little-eye game, picking out farm animals and other items of interest. As the car drew closer to their destination, Rachel grew uneasy. She knew that somehow she had to prepare Holly for the fact that her aunt Lydia might be assuming she was about to get guardianship of her niece.

"I can't wait to meet your aunt Lydia," Rachel began carefully.

"Will she be just like you?"

"Well, no, I don't think so. Maybe she'll be more like your mommy."

"Oh." Holly slowly nodded, as if taking this in.

"And there is a possibility that Aunt Lydia will invite you to live with them."

"On the farm?" Holly turned to peer at Rachel.

"Yes. On the farm."

"You mean for always?"

"It's a possibility." Rachel's hands tightened on the wheel, but she kept her eyes straight forward.

"Would you live with me there?"

"Well . . . no, I mean Aunt Lydia's not my aunt."

"Then I don't want to live there either," Holly declared.

"But it's a farm, Holly. With cows and horses and trees to climb and cousins to play with. You might decide you really like it."

Holly didn't say anything now, but her arms were folded across her front in a stubborn gesture, and her expression seemed to be a mixture of sadness and fear.

"Anyway, I hope that you and I will always be together, Holly."

"Really?" She sounded hopeful.

"Of course." Rachel reached over and smoothed her hand over Holly's hair. "I love you, sweetie. You know that. I love you more than anyone else in the whole wide world."

Holly beamed at her. "I love you too, Aunt Rachel. More than anyone in the whole wide world too. I mean now that Mommy and Daddy are . . . gone."

Rachel felt the lump growing in her throat and was afraid she was about to start crying again, but then, seeing a dark gray buggy ahead with a triangular SLOW sign on the back, she decided to use this as a distraction—for both of them.

"Look, Holly," she said eagerly, slowing the car and pointing down the road. "There's a horse-drawn buggy up there."

"Really?" Holly leaned forward. "There's a horse too?"

"Yes. You'll see it in a minute, when we pass it."

They followed the buggy for a while, and then, seeing there were no other cars coming their way, Rachel eased the car into the other lane and slowly passed the buggy, putting down her window enough to hear the *clip-clop* of the horse's hooves.

"What a pretty horse!" Holly exclaimed.

"It is pretty."

"And look at the funny man and woman," Holly said eagerly. "They're all dressed up like the olden days. Are they going to be in a Christmas program too?"

Rachel remembered the Christmas program at Holly's school before school let out. The children had put on a version of Dickens's *A Christmas Carol*. "No," she said slowly as she pulled in front of the horse-drawn buggy. "Those people dress like that all the time, Holly."

"Why?"

Expecting questions like this, Rachel had done some research on her computer last night, reading up on the Amish, in hopes that she'd begin to understand them better herself. Unfortunately, by the time she'd turned off her computer, she felt more confused than when she'd started. From what she could tell, there were a lot of different kinds of Amish and they didn't all believe and do the same things, although there did seem to be a few commonalities. Perhaps that was all she needed to explain for now.

"The people in that buggy are Amish," she began.

"Amish? What is Amish?"

"Amish is like a religion. Kind of like how we go to church . . . sometimes." Rachel knew this was an understatement, but she had to start somewhere.

"Oh, so they dress up like that to go to church?" Holly nodded as if this made sense. "But is it Sunday?"

"No. It's Saturday. Actually, they dress like that *every* day. The Amish people are kind of old-fashioned. They live the way people lived two hundred years ago."

"Two hundred years ago?"

"Even more probably. The Amish believe it's wrong to use things like electricity or machinery or cars. In fact, that's why you'll see lots of horses and buggies today. It's how they get everywhere."

"They go everywhere in buggies with horses? That would be fun."

"Yes, although it would be slow."

"I wouldn't care if it was slow."

"There's another horse and buggy coming toward us now," Rachel pointed out.

"Will there be lots of horses and buggies?"

"Yes. We're in Amish country now. You'll see lots of buggies and people wearing old-fashioned clothes."

"This is fun."

"And your aunt Lydia and your cousins are Amish too."

"My aunt and cousins are Amish?" Holly's tone grew more excited. "Will they be dressed old-fashioned too?"

"Yes, I'm sure they will, and their house will be different too."

"How will it be different?"

"I'm not sure exactly, but they won't have electricity."

"No electricity? How do they turn on their lights?"

"They have different kinds of lights. Maybe even candles."

"Candles? That sounds like fun."

"Yes, and they don't have phones or computers. Or TV or DVDs." Rachel was well aware that Holly enjoyed her DVD movies. In fact, she suspected that her mini DVD player was in one of the bags, along with some of her kids' DVDs.

"Oh . . ."

"But they have other things to do."

"Like ride horses?" Holly said eagerly.

"Yes. And farm chores."

"Like milk cows?"

"Maybe."

"This is so exciting, Aunt Rachel. We're going to Aunt Lydia's farm and they're going to be like olden-days people."

"Yes . . . it is exciting." However, as she said this, she only felt a fearful sense of foreboding. What if Holly fell in love with the Amish lifestyle? What if she didn't want to go home to Chicago? And, really, could Rachel blame her? What child wouldn't want to live in a beautiful part of the country, on a farm, with horses and cows and cousins? How did Rachel expect to compete with that?

It was late in the afternoon when Rachel turned into the settlement where Aunt Lydia lived. By now the clouds were thick and low overhead, and unless she was mistaken, these clouds would bring snow. At least they'd make it there safely before the first flakes flew, and perhaps it would just be a dusting.

"Walt called your aunt Lydia yesterday," Rachel said as she watched for the Miller mailbox. "To tell her we were coming."

"I thought you said they don't have phones."

"I guess some of them have phones, but not in the houses."

"Oh."

"It's kind of like going back in time," Rachel said. "Like we'll be living in the olden days for a while."

"Will we wear old-fashioned clothes too?" Holly asked eagerly.

"Well, no, I don't think so."

"Oh." Now Holly sounded disappointed.

"There it is!" Rachel pointed to the mailbox with the right address and the name Miller on it. "That's the place." She peered down the graveled road to where a plain white two-story house was situated and, not too far from it, stood a dark red barn—almost like something you'd see in a children's picture book. "Aunt Lydia's farm!"

Holly clapped her hands. "Hurry, hurry."

"I thought you didn't mind going slow," Rachel teased as she turned onto the driveway. "Like the horse and buggy."

"But this is a car."

Rachel parked the little red car in front of the house. She knew it looked out of place and the neighbors might wonder, but she didn't know where else to park it. She had barely turned off the ignition before Holly was out of the car and dashing up to the front door. "Come on, Aunt Rachel," she yelled.

Rachel hurried to join her eager niece, but as she got closer to the porch, she heard angry barking and turned to see a big black dog streaking across the yard toward them. He did not look friendly. Rachel dashed over to grab Holly just as the front door opened.

"Get back, Blue!" a woman wearing a charcoal gray dress shouted at the dog. "Stay." Now she glared at Rachel as if she wasn't expecting visitors. Her faded brown hair was streaked with gray and pulled back into a severe bun that only intensified her harsh expression.

"Hello," Rachel said in a friendly tone. "Is this the Millers'?"

"*Ja.*" The woman nodded briskly, studying them with icy blue eyes. "I am Lydia Miller. This is our farm."

"Did Walt Swanson call you? The attorney from Chicago?"

"Oh, *ja, ja.*" Her expression softened with realization as she turned from Rachel to peer curiously at Holly. "You are Miriam's daughter?" She knelt down, looking intently into Holly's face. "You are little Holly?"

Holly nodded somberly.

Now Lydia put her arms around Holly, holding her tightly.

"Oh, my little lamb," she said. "My poor little lost lamb. *Danki Derr Herr.* You have found your way home."

Rachel just stood there on the porch, shivering as she witnessed the warm familial embrace. In their haste, she'd left her coat in the car, but she noticed that snowflakes were just starting to fly and the icy wind was picking up. The weather was nothing, however, compared to the chill that rushed through her heart just now. She felt certain this was it—she was losing Holly.

Lydia stood now, wiping some tears from her cheeks as she looked over at Rachel. *"Danki, danki."* She smiled, which made her suddenly seem younger. "Thank you for bringing Holly to us. We will take very good care of her. You can be sure of that." She just stood there now, as if waiting for Rachel to leave.

"I'm Holly's other aunt," Rachel said a bit helplessly. She felt dismissed, but wasn't ready to budge.

"Oh?" Lydia looked surprised. "You are her aenti?"

"Yes, I'm Michael's sister. Miri's sister-in-law. Didn't Walt explain all that to you?" Rachel asked.

"I did not understand all that the man told me on the telephone the other day. I was so shocked, so sad, to hear of my sister's death. This morning, my brother, Benjamin—he lives next door—he gave my husband a message. I thought Holly would be delivered to me this week. I did not know she would arrive today."

"Well, if it's too soon, Holly and I can go to a hotel in town and—"

"Oh no, no—it's not too soon. I am glad to have Holly now."

"Oh." Rachel glanced back at her car. "Well, she has a lot of things in the car. I should help her carry them inside and unpack."

"Oh no." Lydia held up her hands. "She has no need for your English things here. We will give her what she needs."

"But she has her toys and clothes and—"

"No, no." Lydia firmly shook her head. "She will not need those."

Holly was looking up at Rachel with a look of fear and insecurity, as if this wasn't how she'd planned this either. Suddenly Rachel knew she could not—she *would* not—despite this strong woman's determination—simply abandon her only niece like this.

"I'm sorry," Rachel began slowly, gathering her thoughts as she spoke. "But Holly has been through a lot. Everything here will be very new to her. If I can't stay here to help her with this transition, she must at least have her things."

"Aunt Rachel?" Holly reached for her hand, imploring with terrified eyes. "You're going to stay here too, *aren't you?*"

"Well, I . . . maybe I should find a hotel in town. But don't worry, I won't leave you—"

"Oh no, no—you do not have to stay in a hotel," Lydia declared. "You will stay here with us for the night."

"If it's no trouble." Rachel felt a small trickle of relief.

"Oh, it is no trouble." She stepped back now, opening the door. "Come in, come in. Welcome to our humble home."

They went into a stark large room, and spying a wood-burning stove in the corner, Rachel went over to it, hoping to thaw herself out a little. Holly stayed right beside her. As she hovered by the heat source, Rachel surveyed the room, taking in the simple wooden chairs, the benches, and a plain-looking side table with a simple wooden clock and several kerosene lanterns on it. Although this room wasn't as stylish or glamorous as Miri and Michael's Chicago apartment, there was a similarity. Probably it was the bare wood floors and the spartan furnishings. Maybe this was where Miri had gotten her sense of style from.

"My husband, Daniel, and the children are working. There is much to be done before the next storm." She paused to light one of the lanterns, then went over to a simple wooden staircase. "I will show you your room. You can put your things in it if you like."

She led them up the dimly lit narrow stairs and down an equally dark and narrow hallway. "The boys sleep in this room." She nodded to a room with three narrow beds. "And this is Sarah's room. You will share with her." She pointed inside a sparse-looking room with only one bed topped with a plain-looking quilt with even blocks of blue and burgundy and gray. Although it appeared to be a full-sized bed, it didn't look big enough for three.

"We all sleep in the same bed?" Holly asked.

"I did not know your aenti was coming to stay." Lydia looked perplexed as she set the lantern on a small wooden dresser. "I will send the boys to the neighbors to borrow a cot for the night."

Rachel thanked her, but wondered if a night in a hotel might not have been the best bet after all. Perhaps it wasn't too late to insist that both she and Holly should spend their first night in a hotel. Maybe that would make for an easier transition for everyone. But by the time they went downstairs, the snow was falling hard and fast and thick, and the idea of driving the little old car back into town during a blizzard was unappealing. Besides, Rachel reminded herself, this was only for one night—and it might even be interesting. But now she needed to come up with a way to pry Holly out of Lydia's eager hands. Hopefully by early in the day tomorrow.

6

Worried that their Amish hostess might go into shock seeing all of Holly's English possessions, Rachel encouraged Holly to leave a lot of her stuff in the car. "Just for the night," Rachel said as she put the bag containing Holly's American Girl doll and clothes back in the trunk. "We can figure it all out better tomorrow."

"But Ivy will be cold and lonely out here," Holly protested.

Rachel shrugged. "Okay, but we can't take it all in. Just take what you really need," she told her. So, loaded down with a lot of bags, they clumped up the stairs and Holly began unpacking some of her bags. Before long, Sarah's sparse little bedroom became cluttered and crowded with fluffy bright-colored items that looked completely out of place—as if they were not truly welcome in this world. Part of Rachel felt guilty about this invasion. Yet another part of her felt like this family might as well see what Holly was accustomed to. Just because Lydia had legal custody of Holly didn't mean she could control who Holly was or who she'd been.

"You're here!" A girl wearing a plain blue dress very similar to Lydia's burst into the room just as they were finishing up. She paused, looking around her room with an astonished expression. "What is all this?"

"My stuff," Holly said. "Are you Sarah? Is this your room?"

"*Ja*. I'm Sarah." She smiled shyly.

"I'm Holly. I'm your cousin."

"I know that. How old are you?"

"I'm six—but I'll be seven on Christmas."

"Your birthday is Christmas?"

"It's the day before Christmas. Christmas Eve," Holly proclaimed proudly.

Sarah nodded with approval. "That is nice."

Holly just shrugged, then pointed to Rachel. "This is Aunt Rachel. Her birthday is three days before mine."

Sarah looked as if she was figuring something in her head. "Is your birthday on Tuesday?" she asked Rachel.

"Yeah, I guess so," Rachel said, not eager to be reminded. Now she smiled at Sarah. "When's your birthday?"

"I just had it. November thirtieth. I turned eleven."

"Wow." Holly looked impressed. "That's pretty old."

"*Ja*. But not as old as my three brothers."

"You have *three* brothers?"

"*Ja*." She held up three fingers, counting them off. "Jacob is the oldest. He's seventeen. And Noah is fifteen. They're both out of school now. Ezra is thirteen. He's still in school like me."

"Wow." Holly looked stunned. "That's a lot of brothers."

"*Ja*. But now I have a sister." Sarah put a loving arm around Holly's shoulders.

"I've always wanted a sister," Holly said, but she gave Rachel a sideways glance, as if she was unsure.

68

"You have got one now," Sarah proclaimed. Then she frowned at all of Holly's stuff. "But Mamm will not be happy to see all this."

"Who is Mamm?"

"Mamm?" Sarah's brow creased. "Our mother. That's Mamm."

"Oh."

"Amish use some different words," Rachel explained to Holly.

"*Ja*. We speak English mostly, but we also speak the Dutch."

"Which is a form of German," Rachel explained and then wondered why she'd bothered. So much for Holly to take in. Why add to it?

"And what do you call your father?" Holly asked with adultlike interest.

"We call him Daed."

"I called my daddy Dad sometimes. But mostly I called him Daddy."

"I'm sorry that your parents died," Sarah said with a serious expression. "I never met my aenti Miriam. She was Mamm's only sister, and Mamm thinks I look like her."

Holly peered at Sarah, looking her up and down, but then she just shook her head. "No. My mother was older and bigger than you."

Rachel chuckled. "I think she means her coloring. See, Sarah has golden brown hair like your mommy did. And her eyes are the same color of blue."

"Oh." Holly nodded. "I guess you do look like Mommy. Maybe she looked like you when she was a little girl." Holly reached over to take Rachel's hand. "My mommy says I look like Aunt Rachel." She smiled up at her. "That's right, isn't it?"

"That's what your mommy used to say," Rachel said quietly.

Sarah spotted Holly's American Girl doll and pointed at it with a shocked expression while her other hand flew up to cover her mouth. "Mamm is not going to like *that*."

Holly grabbed up Ivy with the possessiveness of a protective mother. "Why not? What's wrong with her?"

Sarah pointed at Ivy's face. "She has a *face*."

Holly frowned in confusion. "What's wrong with her face?"

Sarah giggled nervously. "I have to go help Mamm fix supper."

Holly still looked perplexed.

"We'll make sure Ivy stays up in the bedroom," Rachel assured Sarah. "I hope that's okay."

Sarah looked unsure, but she nodded. "Mamm told me to ask if you need anything." She looked around the crowded room and laughed. "It looks like you don't need *anything*."

"I need to use the bathroom," Holly admitted as she carefully laid Ivy down next to Bunny.

Sarah showed them where the bathroom was, and Rachel was relieved to learn this house had indoor plumbing. "How does it work?" she asked Sarah.

"What do you mean?" Sarah asked with a confused expression. "You have not used a flushing toilet before?"

Rachel laughed. "Yes, I have, but I'm just curious about how you have water pressure without electricity. Is there a pump to get water to the house?"

Sarah's brow creased. "There is a windmill that makes

power to get water up into the water tower." She held her hand up high as if to illustrate the height. "And then the water tower uses *gravity* to get it into the house." She dropped her hand down as if to explain how gravity worked. Then as if to further explain, she turned on the tap. "See?"

"Really?" Rachel was impressed. "That's very clever."

Sarah looked at Rachel as if she questioned her sensibilities, but instead she simply pointed out the lanterns hanging on the wall. "These are for *light*. So you can *see*." Now she pointed to the matches on a nearby shelf. "You use *these* to light them with." Then, shaking her head, Sarah went on downstairs. Thankfully, she did not take the time to explain the towels or the toilet tissue to Rachel.

Holly giggled as she picked up the box of matches. "I'm not supposed to play with these," she told Rachel.

"I know." Rachel frowned as she took the matchbox from Holly. "Let me light the lanterns for you."

"I like how this kind of light looks," Holly said as the lantern flickered to life. "It's all fuzzy and warm, don't you think?"

Rachel looked at Holly, sweetly illuminated in the soft golden light. "Yes, it is kind of fuzzy and warm." She shivered slightly as the chill of the house ran through her. "And fuzzy and warm can be very good."

Rachel felt uneasy and slightly intrusive as she and Holly went downstairs. She could hear quiet voices in the kitchen and felt the polite thing to do would be to go in and offer to help, but she had no idea how this would be received.

"Should we see if Aunt Lydia needs help?" she asked Holly.

Holly nodded. She'd carried Bunny down with her but looked uncertain now. "Should I leave Bunny here?"

Rachel agreed. "Yes. She probably won't be much help in the kitchen."

Holly set Bunny in a chair, then took Rachel's hand and together they walked into the kitchen. "Excuse me," Rachel said politely. "Is there something we can do to help?"

Rachel was relieved when Lydia found several simple tasks that needed doing, and soon both Rachel and Holly were busily helping. Rachel could tell that having unexpected guests for dinner had probably put some extra pressure on their hostess tonight. At least they appeared to have plenty of food. As Rachel smelled the pork roast cooking, she realized she was actually quite hungry.

It wasn't long until everyone was finding their places at a long wooden table illuminated by a large kerosene lantern that hung from the ceiling. Although it was a simple meal with mismatched dishes on a bare wood table, it felt surprisingly festive due to the flickering golden light. Rachel and Holly were told to sit with Sarah on a bench that ran along one side, and the three boys sat on the bench on the opposite side. Then Daniel came in and, without saying a word, sat at the head of the table.

"Good evening," Rachel said in a friendly tone, trying not to stare at his odd-looking beard.

"*Gut-n-owed*," Daniel said to her.

Lydia set the last of the serving bowls in the center of the table, taking her seat at the opposite end of the table. She took a moment to introduce everyone, and afterward Daniel bowed his head, as did the rest of his family. Rachel nudged Holly, hinting that she should imitate their host too. She waited for him to ask a blessing on the food, but no words were uttered. Instead, everyone just kept their heads bowed, with no one saying anything. All Rachel could hear was the ticking of a clock somewhere.

Eventually Holly's head popped up, but Rachel sent her a quick sideways warning glance, tipping her head to signal Holly to keep her head bowed. She wasn't sure what was going on here, but she didn't want to be impolite or disrespectful. Finally, after what seemed an awfully long time, Daniel said "amen," and just like that, the table sprang back to life in an almost other-worldly sort of way.

It wasn't so much that they were a chatty bunch, but it was clear from the activity that they were all hungry. They'd probably been working hard; plus it was cold outside. As food was passed and served and shuffled about, a few bits and pieces of farm information were exchanged around the table, as well as some thoughts about the weather and the forecast. It sounded as if this snowstorm was expected to last a few days. Rachel hoped they were wrong about that. She told them about the good driving weather she and Holly had enjoyed today. However, no one seemed interested to hear more. In fact, no one seemed terribly interested in the two virtual strangers sharing the table with them. Perhaps this was their way of being polite and unobtrusive, or maybe they were just too hungry to express interest in anything but the food.

Yet, as hungry as this family appeared, no one gobbled down their food. No one was in a hurry. Instead, they were content to savor and enjoy the meal, and Rachel thought that was admirable. Too often, she saw people rushing to eat. It was refreshing to witness a family all sitting together and enjoying a meal. It reminded her of some of the old television shows she used to enjoy on TV—shows like *The Waltons* or *Little House on the Prairie*. Although it was hard to believe that people actually lived like this, she knew they were not putting this act on for her benefit.

Eventually the meal ended, and Rachel and Holly remained in the kitchen to help Lydia and Sarah. Thanks to the number of dishes and the absence of things like a dishwasher, the cleanup was far more tedious than Rachel was used to. When they were finally done, though, there was a good sense of accomplishment to see that all the counters were clear and clean and the dishes were all put away.

"Do you like to play games?" Sarah asked Holly.

Holly's eyes lit up. "Yes! I have Nintendo in the car and I have—"

"I don't think Sarah means video games," Rachel quickly explained.

"Oh?" Holly nodded with a perplexed expression, almost as if she were a tourist in a foreign country, trying to figure out a completely different culture.

"Sarah probably means board games. Like Chutes and Ladders."

"I like those games too," Holly said with renewed enthusiasm.

The game Sarah set up appeared to be similar to Chinese checkers. It involved a handmade wooden board and colored marbles, and it didn't take long before Holly got the hang of it. It also didn't take long before the two restless older boys disappeared. According to Sarah, they'd probably gone out to the barn to "horse around." Ezra remained behind, whittling on a piece of wood and eventually joining in the marbles game. Meanwhile, Daniel tended to the fire and read from a serious-looking brown book. If anyone was curious about their houseguests, they were doing a good job of keeping it to themselves. Perhaps this was simply Amish etiquette.

Rachel had brought her ebook reader with her, and it had a fully charged battery, but she was uncertain about getting it out. She didn't want to insult anyone with her technology. Instead, she decided to just sit and soak in all this quiet activity. After all, when would she have an experience like this again?

Seeing the children down on the floor—two who appeared to be from another century playing with Holly, who was dressed in a bright plaid jumper with lime green leggings—made for an interesting scene. Rachel almost wished she had her camera, and yet she'd heard the Amish didn't care to be photographed. She was glad that the children were including Holly and were having fun. After a bit, Lydia joined them in the front room. She had a sewing basket in hand, and with nothing more than a nod in Rachel's direction, she settled herself onto the high-backed bench near the fire and began to work on mending what appeared to be a pair of trousers. It was all a very homey scene, albeit quiet, and Rachel was determined to enjoy it.

Because, Rachel assured herself, by tomorrow night if all went well, she and Holly would be back in the Chicago apartment and this would be only a memory. It was surprising how the apartment suddenly sounded far more inviting than ever before. She actually missed it. Oh, it wasn't that Rachel didn't know how to rough it a little. It was simply that she didn't quite understand the reasoning behind these rustic deprivations. Sure, it was fun, in a going-back-in-time sort of way, but as a full-time lifestyle? Perhaps she could understand why Miri had left all this behind her, although it did make Rachel curious too. It was so mysterious to think her modern-minded sister-in-law had grown up in this sort of quaint atmosphere. Perhaps while she was here, she would learn a bit more about Miri's previous life. For Holly's sake, she hoped so.

It wasn't too long until Lydia announced it was time for the children to get ready for bed, but as she and Holly went up to Sarah's room, Rachel realized there was still only one bed. She was about to go downstairs and inquire about this when she heard the boisterous voices of the older boys as they clomped up the stairs, and just like that, a rollaway cot was set down next to the bed. This was followed by a set of bedding carried in by Sarah and Lydia.

"Here you are," Lydia said as she placed the folded blankets and things in Rachel's arms. Rachel thanked them and began to make up the narrow bed.

Now Lydia went over to where Sarah was watching Holly removing her pajamas from her backpack. "And do not forget we have church in the morning, *maed*."

Sarah nodded. "*Ja*, Mamm. I know."

"*Schlaf gut*," Lydia said. Then she gave Rachel an uneasy glance and exited the room. Unsure of what Lydia had said, Rachel told her good night and continued wrestling with the cot.

Wearing a long white nightgown, Sarah came over to check her progress. "I can sleep on the cot, if you want to sleep with Holly in my bed," she offered generously.

"But I want to sleep with *you*, Sarah," Holly insisted as

she tugged on her pink Hello Kitty pajama top. "Aunt Rachel can sleep on the cot."

Rachel tried not to feel slighted by this surprising preference, but suddenly it was like Rachel was in grade school again, being pushed aside by one friend for another. Still, as she slipped into her own silky pajamas, by herself in the bathroom, since it felt strange to dress in front of the young girls, she decided that her reaction was perfectly silly. Besides, she would rather sleep alone.

Like little girls at a sleepover, Sarah and Holly had some trouble settling down for the night, and eventually, Holly begged Rachel to read to them from her favorite bedtime storybook. "It will help me go to sleep," Holly pointed out.

"I can read it to you," Sarah offered kindly.

"Okay," Holly gladly agreed. "I'll bet you're a good reader."

And so, for the second time that night, Rachel felt slightly displaced . . . or replaced. But, once again, she told herself it was perfectly ridiculous. She should be happy for Holly's sake. How fun for her to have this special night with her cousin. She hoped that's all it was. Just a one-night sleepover. Somehow, they had to get out of this place by tomorrow. Rachel was determined.

After the girls had finally drifted off to sleep, and the rest of the house grew quiet—as in *completely quiet*—Rachel became unbearably restless. Tossing and turning on the lumpy cot, she knew she was never going to be able to go to sleep. Normally, she would get out of bed and read until she was sleepy when she felt like this, but she didn't want to get up and stumble around the very dark house. Yet the idea of lighting one of those lanterns and creeping around was equally unsettling, so she remained in the uncomfortable little bed with all her uncomfortable big thoughts and desperately hoped that morning would come quickly. This was what came from getting that last coffee when she'd filled up with gas just before coming here. The caffeine was playing havoc with her nerves.

After a while, she realized her anxiety was not related to the double espresso as much as to plain old fear. The truth was she was scared to death. She'd been trying to be positive, hoping for the best, but underneath it all, she was afraid she was really going to lose Holly. In fact, it already felt like she was losing her—and they'd only been here a few hours.

She couldn't even imagine what tomorrow would be like. Lydia had made it clear they had church in the morning. Rachel knew that Lydia expected Holly to go with them—and she suspected that Lydia wanted Rachel to be on her way by then. How could Rachel possibly leave Holly behind? Why hadn't Michael and Miri considered the consequences of their poorly thought out decision to do this? How dare they go and die, leaving Holly's life hanging in the balance like this? As much as Rachel missed them and wished they were still here, she also felt very angry with them, infuriated by their shortsightedness . . . and their selfishness. Their foolishness was going to cost Holly and Rachel everything.

Finally, feeling totally helpless, Rachel knew the only thing she could do, the only power she really had, was to pray, and so she asked God to intervene on her behalf. "Please, make Lydia understand that I need Holly and that Holly needs me. Let us be on our way out of here first thing in the morning." She prayed this silently but fervently—and several times for emphasis. As she said "amen," she believed God was listening, and that he was going to be merciful.

When she got up the next morning, she looked out the window to see a thick blanket of snow on the ground. She knew that driving all the way back to Chicago in the Karmann Ghia was no longer an option. She also knew that the closest airport was probably in Cleveland. The Karmann Ghia wouldn't be safe for that long of a trip either. Not in this weather. Even if it was a risk she could take for herself, she wouldn't think of taking it for Holly. For the time being she seemed stuck here . . . but maybe that was a good thing.

7

Once again, Rachel got dressed in the privacy of the bathroom, but when she came out she saw that Ezra and Noah were waiting. Despite their blank expressions, she could see the impatience in their stances and suspected that there were time limits for using the only bathroom.

"I'm sorry," she told them as she hurried out with her pale pink pajamas bundled in her arms. When she got back to Sarah's bedroom, she was surprised to see that Holly's dress was still lying on the bed. "Why aren't you dressed?" Rachel picked up the green velvet Christmas dress. She had felt this was the most acceptable thing for church, but there was Holly wearing what looked like a white slip and long black stockings, and Sarah, already dressed, was pulling a cornflower blue dress over Holly's head.

"What are you doing?" Rachel asked as she laid her pajamas on the cot. "Why aren't you wearing your own dress, Holly?"

"Sarah and Aunt Lydia got me an Amish dress to wear," Holly said proudly. "I get to dress like them today, Aunt Rachel." She spun around to show off her long dress. "Isn't it beautiful?"

Sarah giggled. "It's not beautiful, Holly. It's plain. And plain is good."

"Well, I think it's beautiful too," Holly insisted.

"Now hold still while I pin the apron on," Sarah instructed.

To Rachel's horror, Sarah had a bunch of straight pins, the kind Rachel's mother had once used for sewing, and was pinning the white apron and some sort of shawl over the dress. "What are you doing?" Rachel asked.

"Pinning her apron and cape," Sarah explained.

"But those pins—they'll poke her." Rachel felt angry. Not only did the cotton dress look too cool for winter, it was unsafe to secure those other pieces with straight pins. "I really don't think you should pin it like that. It looks dangerous."

"No, she will be fine," Sarah assured her. She looked at Rachel with clear blue eyes but a confused expression. "We *always* pin our clothes like this." She turned around to show Rachel her own apron and cape. "See?"

"But don't the pins poke you?"

"No." Sarah made a tolerant smile, as if she were reassuring a child. "If you pin them right, you are fine." She showed her how it was done, but Rachel still felt skeptical. She'd never heard of pinning clothing on to a child like that.

"Sarah," Rachel said firmly, "I do *not* want Holly to get hurt by these ridiculous pins. What if a pin slips out and stabs her?"

"That will *not* happen." Lydia's figure shadowed the doorway. "Sarah knows how to pin clothes properly. You need not trouble yourself, Rachel."

Rachel frowned at her. "But it seems unsafe."

"It is how we do it here. It is how we have done it for generations." Lydia, predictably, was dressed identically to Sarah and Holly. Even her dress was blue, although it was darker.

"But why?"

Lydia gave her an exasperated expression. "We do not have time for this now." Lydia looked carefully at Holly as if inspecting her. "The dress is good on her," she told Sarah. "And it is good that Holly's shoes are black, but they are not plain enough."

Rachel wanted to ask why everything had to be so dog-goned plain but knew she wouldn't get an answer.

"Come, come," Lydia said. "Hurry and be ready, *maed*. It is time for breakfast and then we go to church."

Rachel watched as Sarah continued with Holly, brushing her hair back and struggling to put it into a very short pony-tail. "I don't think there's enough here yet to make a bun," Sarah told her. "But it will grow . . . in time." She made a *tsk-tsk* sound. "A girl should never cut her hair." She reached to the dresser for a white bonnet that looked just like the one she was wearing. "Now, for your *kapp*."

"My cap?" Holly tilted her head to one side.

"Hold still," Sarah insisted as she secured the *kapp* to Holly's head. Thankfully she did not use straight pins to do this. Instead, she used four large bobby pins and seemed to know exactly how to do it. "There," she said proudly. "You are ready."

Holly looked at Rachel now. "What about you?"

Rachel held up her hands. "What do you mean—what about me?"

"Where's *your* Amish dress, Aunt Rachel? Sarah says that to go to Amish church you must wear an Amish dress."

Rachel shrugged. "Then I guess I won't be going to church today."

Holly frowned. "But you *have* to go."

Rachel shook her head but was secretly relieved. Some alone time was sounding good right now. "I'm sorry, Holly. I just don't see how I can go without a dress. You'll have to go without me, but when you get back you must promise to tell me all about it. Okay?"

"Okay." Holly nodded with uncertainty.

"Now we must hurry to eat breakfast," Sarah instructed, and taking Holly's hand, she hurried out of the room and down the stairs.

Rachel grabbed up Holly's fur-trimmed scarlet hood and headed downstairs too. She chuckled at the bright coat. At least *that* would show some of Holly's individuality!

Breakfast was oatmeal, but thankfully there was coffee too. Without saying anything to Lydia, Rachel helped herself to a cup, then almost wished she hadn't. Did they really drink this stuff? After doctoring it with cream and sugar, which she normally wouldn't do, she went to the table and sat down next to Holly. Sarah was nearly done with her oatmeal, but Holly was picking at hers, and Rachel knew it wasn't the kind Holly was used to.

"Daniel and the boys have gone next door to set up the benches," Lydia told Rachel as she set a bowl of oatmeal in front of her.

"The benches?" Rachel looked down at the clumpy oatmeal and wondered if she was really hungry.

"For church," Sarah explained. "It's at Mammi's barn today."

"Mammi's barn?" Holly questioned. "Who is Mammi and why is church in a barn and not in a church?"

"Mammi is your grandmother," Sarah told her.

"I have a grandmother?" Holly's eyes grew large.

"*Ja.* She was your mudder's mudder and mine too," Lydia explained. "And church is always in a barn, Holly. Everyone takes turns having it. The men go early to set up benches. Usually we go in the buggy, but today is good because we can walk. We do not need to harness up the horse."

Holly looked disappointed. "No horse and buggy?" she asked.

"Not today, *liebschen.*" Lydia smiled. "Another day we will go in the buggy."

Holly poked at her oatmeal.

"You do not like oatmeal?" Lydia asked.

"She's used to a different kind," Rachel told her.

"Oh . . ." Lydia went to a cupboard. "I know how to make her like it." She quickly returned with a jar of brown sugar and a square of butter. "Try it like this, Holly."

To Rachel's surprise, Holly loved the improved oatmeal. Rachel was glad to see she was getting something solid in her tummy, but still, she felt dismayed . . . as if she was steadily losing her.

"Sarah tells me you are not going to church," Lydia said to Rachel, but Rachel could tell by the gleam in Lydia's eyes that she was pleased with this news. "And that is best, I think. You will want to get an early start on your travels."

"My travels?"

Lydia's heavy, dark brows arched. "*Ja.* You are going home today, *recht?*"

Rachel waved her hand toward the bare window, wondering why none of their windows had curtains—just one more thing she did not understand. "I don't really see how I can drive in all that snow."

"Oh, that is nothing, that snow. You can drive in it just fine."

"Have you seen our car?" Rachel asked. "It's not exactly made for these kind of driving conditions."

"Surely your car can drive through a little snow." Lydia looked unimpressed. "And the main road will be better, I think."

Rachel didn't want to go into all the reasons why she couldn't drive back to Chicago this morning—primarily because she was not ready to abandon her only niece. She decided that if there were things Lydia didn't have time to explain—like why one pinned clothing on to young children—then perhaps she shouldn't expect Rachel to explain why she didn't want to drive a little old sports car over dangerous snowy roads.

Fortunately, Lydia didn't pursue this topic further. Instead, she hurried the girls through breakfast, then insisted it was time to go. When Rachel went to get Holly's red coat, however, Lydia held up her hands. "No, no, that will not do." Instead, she pulled out a dark gray sort of cloak, wrapping it around Holly. It didn't seem very substantial.

"But you're going to be in a barn," Rachel pointed out. "Will she be warm enough in that? Her parka is down-filled, and that cotton dress is thin."

"She will be good," Lydia said. "It is how we do it here." She locked eyes with Rachel now, as if inviting her to challenge this.

Rachel just sighed. "Well, she'd better not come down with pneumonia or I'll be taking her straight back to Chicago with me. Even if we have to charter a plane to get there."

Lydia's eyes flashed, but instead of responding, she just played the part of a mother hen, ushering the girls out of the kitchen. "Hurry, hurry. We do not want to be late, *kinder*."

The house grew very quiet with everyone gone, and for a long time, Rachel just sat at the dining table, gazing out the window over the vast white snowy fields with occasional trees and other homesteads and barns to break it up. It was truly beautiful . . . peaceful . . . bucolic . . . serene. This would be a lovely location for a home—that is, if it were a more modern home and not smack in the middle of this weird Amish community.

She could imagine a comfortable house with central heat and appliances and a TV or source of music, as well as a few of the other modern comforts. And perhaps instead of the plain woodstove, it would have a tall stone fireplace with a crackling fire. Thinking of this reminded her of how Daniel had kept the fire going last night. She wondered if she should do something to keep it going now. She wasn't very familiar with woodstoves, but it seemed simple enough to put a piece or two of wood in it. Finding only a few sticks of wood in the woodbox next to it, she carefully opened the door and, seeing only red coals, decided to slip these last pieces in. It was better than nothing. Besides, if the fire ran out, it seemed that the house would chill down significantly. She'd have thought these practical-minded people would've thought of this. However, they seemed somewhat oblivious to their own comfort. Their furniture was hard, their clothes were funny, and their bathroom . . . well, she didn't even want to get thinking on the fact that a family of six, and their two guests who made eight, shared one single bathroom.

Satisfied with her initiative to keep from freezing, she decided to go make herself useful by finishing the cleaning up in the kitchen. She knew that Lydia had started on it, but there were still some dishes and the oatmeal pan to be washed. By now, Rachel knew how to work the pump at the sink. And she knew the big kettle of hot water on the stove was for washing dishes. Hard work to be certain, but perhaps it would help justify her free room and board if she helped whenever she could. She did not want to feel beholden to Lydia. The fact of the matter was she didn't much care for Lydia. And she knew that Lydia did not care for her. Lydia would probably like nothing better than to come home to find the red Karmann Ghia gone from the driveway and Rachel far away on her "travels," even if that meant totaling the car or ending up in a ditch.

By the time she had the kitchen cleaned, nearly an hour had passed. Still feeling chilled in the less than cozy house, she decided to go off in search of more firewood. Surely, with all these guys around, there had to be a nice supply somewhere. She got her coat and boots, which weren't really snow boots, but at least they went above her ankles. She went outside and set out to find the firewood.

Of course, she was barely out the door before the big black dog raced toward her, but at least he wasn't barking this time. Not very familiar with farm dogs, she didn't know what to expect. "Hello, Blue," she said in a friendly voice when he stopped right in front of her. She held out her hand with the palm down so he could sniff. She thought she'd read somewhere that was how to befriend a dog. His tail began to wag and she considered that a positive sign. "Good dog," she said as she carefully patted his head, then scratched his ear, which he seemed to appreciate. "You're a good old boy, aren't you? Just protecting your family." She stood up and looked around. "Do you happen to know where they keep the wood?"

He followed her with interest as she walked around searching for a woodshed; then spying a small outbuilding near the kitchen side of the house, she went over to investigate. Upon opening the door, she was surprised to discover it was actually an outhouse. Okay, so she'd been wrong—this house had one and a half baths. Not that she'd call this a half—more like a fourth—although it *was* a two-seater. Then getting a whiff of something less than pleasant, she slammed the wood door shut and hurriedly backed away. She hoped to never be desperate enough to have to use that.

She looked over to the barn. Was it possible they kept their firewood in there? Since there was a nicely shoveled trail leading from the back porch to the barn, she decided to go find out. On the way she could see tracks leading away from there, and she assumed it must've been how the family had gotten to the neighboring farm, where apparently Holly's grandmother lived. Rachel was curious to meet Miri's mother, and she wondered if a mother might be curious to hear about her daughter's adult life—or even more, about how she'd died. It seemed only natural.

She and Blue were nearly to the barn and just walking past what looked like a watering trough, when—just like that—her feet went flying out from under her and she found herself lying flat on her back with the wind knocked out of her. Ice! Shocked and embarrassed as Blue curiously looked down on her, she did at least feel grateful that he was the only witness. She remained motionless on the ground, taking inventory of her limbs and deciding nothing was broken. About to sit up, she heard the sound of footsteps crunching in the snow.

"Are you all right?" a deep voice inquired.

Feeling self-conscious for her clumsiness, she sat up and looked to see a man dressed in an outfit very similar to what Daniel and the boys had been wearing yesterday, standing next to Blue and peering down on her. "That was quite a fall. Did you hurt anything?" Unlike Daniel, this man's face was clean shaven, with no funny-looking beard, and below the wide brim of his black felt hat, she spied thick dark hair, peppered with gray. She wondered about his age and suspected he was older than Miri—maybe late thirties. However, it was the eyes that captivated her. Warm and brown, they twinkled with concern mixed with curiosity.

"You mean besides my pride?" She frowned.

"No broken bones?"

"I don't think so."

He extended a hand and she gratefully grasped it, but as soon as she was on her feet, she started slipping around on the slick surface, and he actually had to grab hold of her to keep her from going down again.

"There's quite an ice rink right here," he said as he guided her to safer ground. "Someone left the trough water running last night and it overflowed and froze."

"I should've been more careful." She extracted herself from

him, brushing the snow and ice off of her slightly dampened backside.

"What are you doing out here anyway?" he asked.

"Looking for firewood."

"Firewood?" He reached up and scratched his chin. "Out in the barn?"

"Well, I couldn't find any around the house and the wood-stove was about to go out. So I thought—"

"How about if I show you where they hide it," he said.

"They *hide* it?"

He chuckled. "Sorry. Just kidding."

She turned to peer at him as he led her back toward the house. Was he really Amish, and, if so, why wasn't he as solemn and serious as the others? "Who are you anyway?" she asked. Suddenly she imagined a scene from a scary movie—the kind where the guy befriends the lone woman and then instead of helping her find firewood, he comes at her wielding an ax and a wicked smile.

"I'm Benjamin Schrock."

"Oh?" The name was vaguely familiar but didn't exactly ring a bell.

"Miriam's brother." He peered curiously at her. "And you're Rachel Milligan, Michael Milligan's sister and Miriam's sister-in-law and Holly's aunt." He sighed. "I'm sorry for your loss, Rachel."

She blinked, as much taken aback by his knowledge of her identity as she was with his sympathy. She suddenly felt close to tears. "Well, yes . . . I'm sorry for your loss too, Benjamin." She turned to study him. "You're really Miri's brother?"

He just nodded.

She watched him closely as they walked back toward the house. Although his hair was dark, his eyes seemed similar to Miri's and something about his profile felt familiar too.

"I still can't believe she's gone," he said as he led her over to what looked like a rectangular igloo covered in snow. He brushed some snow off the top of what appeared to be a box, then flipped open the lid to reveal rows of neatly stacked firewood. *"Voilà."*

"Voilà?" She peered curiously at him. "That's not exactly an Amish word."

He laughed. "There are all kinds of Amish, Rachel."

She smiled, thinking that was actually something of a relief. Maybe there was more to the Amish than she realized. She reached into the box for a piece of wood.

"Here, let me help." He stuck out his arms like a rack. "Go ahead and load me up."

She layered on a fairly hefty load of firewood, and then satisfied, she closed the lid and they both walked into the house together, where she unloaded the pieces one by one into the woodbox by the fireplace. Before she could get to it, Benjamin opened the woodstove, and after stirring the coals with a poker, he inserted several good-sized pieces of wood, then slammed the door shut and adjusted some sort of knob. "There, that should keep the place good and warm until church is over."

"How long does church last?"

He looked over at the clock by the stairs. "At least another hour or so. And then they will stay longer to eat afterward. Are you going to go over and join them for lunch?"

She shrugged uncomfortably. "I, uh, I don't think so."

He frowned. "Meaning Lydia didn't invite you?"

She shrugged again.

"Well, I know my mother—Miriam's mother—wants to meet you."

She waved her hands as if to show her clothing. "I don't have the right attire to go over there."

He made an exasperated sigh. "You're not Amish, Rachel. No one expects you to change your appearance in order to mix with the Amish. That's ridiculous."

"Really?" She frowned. "That's not the impression I got."

He shook his head. "Don't mind Lydia. I heard that her nose is out of joint because you're here." He glanced around the room. "By the way, where's Holly? I'd love to meet my niece."

"Lydia took her to church." Rachel grimaced. "After Sarah dressed her up like a little Amish doll."

"And you don't approve?" He tipped his head to one side.

"I don't know how I feel exactly." She bit her lip, wondering how much to say to Lydia's brother. Was he really to be trusted? "So . . . why aren't *you* at church?" she asked impertinently.

He looked down, plucked some wood slivers from his jacket sleeve, and dropped them into the firewood box. "I came over here to check on a cow that's fixed to calve. It's what I'd call an unplanned pregnancy." He chuckled. "Meaning it's pretty early in the winter for birthing calves, but sometimes nature just takes its own road." He smiled at her and his eyes twinkled. "But it was nice to meet you, Rachel. Now if you'll excuse me, I want to make sure Buttercup is all right. I'm not sure if she's going to drop this calf today or tomorrow, but I know it won't be long now."

"Sure," she said. "And thanks for helping me." The little girl inside of her wanted to ask if she could go with him to the barn and admit she'd never seen the birthing of a calf before and that it sounded interesting—but the stubborn grown-up inside of her dug her heels in. She was not going to let anyone or anything pull her into this backward Amish world. The more she disliked it, the harder she would work to save Holly from getting stuck here.

8

Rachel stood in front of the fire for a while in an attempt to dry out her jeans that had gotten dampened on her unexpected fall. She wished she would've packed another pair of pants now. Although she'd brought along an extra sweater and shirt, she had planned to make these jeans last the day or two she'd expected to be here. Perhaps she hadn't thought things through well enough.

With her jeans dried, she started pacing back and forth in the living room, trying to think of a strategy—a way to get Holly out of here before it was too late—when she heard the front door creak open. She jumped, turning to see that it was Benjamin again.

"Sorry to startle you," he said. "But I thought I should take you over to have some lunch and to meet Mamm."

"Oh?"

"Come on," he urged. "No one really cares how you're dressed. It's not like they think you're Amish."

"You're sure?"

"*Ja.* Get your coat and come on."

Soon they were trekking over the path that had been made earlier. The snow was getting inside her boots, but she was more concerned with how the snow would've gotten into Holly's shoes and whether she was warm enough in that thin dress and shawl. She had been completely serious about her threat to get a plane to fly Holly out of here if she got sick.

"You seem deep in thought," Benjamin said.

"Oh—sorry." She looked over at him. "I'm just worried about Holly."

"Why?"

She let her guard down, explaining about how Holly's clothes seemed inappropriate and how the pins bothered her and how her shoes were probably all soggy from the snow.

"I wouldn't be too concerned. Those black stockings the girls wear are pretty thick and warm and they have lots of layers of under-things beneath those dresses." He chuckled. "Trust me, I was the only brother of three sisters."

"*Three* sisters?"

"*Ja.* Ruth lives in a settlement a few miles from here."

"Does she know about Miri?"

"*Ja.* Everyone knows, Rachel. This is a small world here."

"Oh."

"Mamm has probably taken Miriam's death harder than anyone." He sighed. "Although it's been difficult for all of us. I think every one of us feels somewhat responsible."

"Responsible for her death?" Rachel was confused.

"I mean responsible that she left the settlement. As senseless as that may seem, it probably makes us feel somewhat responsible for her death too."

"Oh." Rachel shivered, pulling her scarf more snugly

around her neck. However, she wasn't sure if it was the temperature that had chilled her just now . . . or his words.

"Anyway, what I'm trying to say is that Mamm is not exactly herself. My father died last spring, which is why I'm helping with the farm. But this news about Miriam—well, it's been hard on her."

"I'm sorry."

"I was hoping you might be able to say something to encourage her."

"Right . . . well, I'll do what I can."

He pointed to a red barn that was very similar to the Millers' barn. "That's where they are. It sounds like they're already having lunch. It's a pretty casual affair. Mostly just sandwiches." He grinned at her. "How do you feel about peanut butter and marshmallow cream?"

"What—that's a sandwich?"

He nodded. "It's one of the favorites."

"Holly will probably love it."

He was leading her toward a door that was partly open, and she could see lots of people, all dressed just like the Millers and Holly had been dressed, milling about. Women seemed clustered on one side and men on the other. Some were eating. Some were talking. And some of the younger children, including Holly, she noticed, were running around and playing a game of tag or hide-n-seek or something. The barn was warmer than she expected and the general atmosphere was surprisingly cheerful. She knew she should be relieved, but once again, she resented this. She wanted to find them all sitting solemnly with hands folded and the children fidgeting, and she wanted Holly to complain and say she wanted to go home—home to Chicago. But right now Holly was chasing a boy around the hay bales, stacked like bleachers in the back of the barn. This was a children's paradise.

"Mamm is over there." He led her past a food table, with a couple other rough-board-and-sawhorse tables nearby. Sitting at one of them were a number of elderly looking women.

"Mamm," Benjamin began gently, "I want you to meet Rachel Milligan. Michael Milligan was her brother."

"I know who she is," the older woman told him a bit sharply.

"This is my mother, Mrs. Schrock," Benjamin told her as he pulled over a folding chair, setting it down next to his mother, who was dressed in black, and patting on it for Rachel to sit. "I'll get you a sandwich," he offered as she sat.

She almost told him not to bother, except that she'd barely touched the oatmeal and her stomach was starting to growl. She turned to the gray-haired woman. "I'm pleased to meet you, Mrs. Schrock."

"Your brother was married to Miriam?" Mrs. Schrock peered curiously at her.

"Yes, and my brother loved your daughter very much. They were very happy together."

"I met young Holly." She nodded. "She is a sweet child."

"Yes, I agree."

"Thank you for bringing her to us."

Rachel looked down at her hands in her lap and wished for the right words. Instead, she struggled to hold back tears. It was just too hard being considered the delivery person—as if they thought she could simply transport her niece and then leave.

"God has given us a second chance with Holly."

Rachel looked up, taking in some quick breaths and hoping to hold her tears at bay. "A second chance?"

"Because we lost Miriam. God has given us Holly . . . in return."

Rachel looked directly at her, staring into the faded blue eyes. "I lost my only brother and I lost Miri, my only sister-in-law, and now I am losing Holly." Her voice broke. "What is God giving *me* in return?" And then to her embarrassment, the tears began to pour out. "Excuse me," she said in a choked tone. With blurry eyes, she hurried through the crowded space and rushed outside, following the path back to the Miller house. She ran inside and up the stairs and into Sarah's room, where she lay down on the narrow cot and allowed her tears to flow freely.

Fortunately, she was recovered by the time the family came home. Even more fortunately, Holly was completely oblivious to her aunt's public breakdown. However, she noticed Sarah looking curiously at her and she supposed someone had mentioned it to her . . . and Lydia. Just the same, Rachel held her head up and tried to act as if nothing was wrong. When it came time to prepare supper, she joined Lydia in the kitchen, trying hard to make herself useful. But this time, something in her was changed. Whether it was having been humbled or feeling defeated, she felt as though she'd lost something today . . . and she wasn't sure she could get it back.

Supper was very much like supper had been last night, except that this time, neither Holly nor Rachel was caught off guard by the long silent blessing before the meal. Although Rachel tried to appear pleasant, she said very little as they ate, feeling as if she was biding her time. She wasn't even sure why. Afterward, she offered to help in the kitchen again.

"Aunt Rachel, do you still want me to tell you all about church?" Holly asked as the four females worked together.

With her hands in the soapy dishwater, since she was washing tonight, Rachel tried to toss her niece a warning glance, as if to say, "later," but Holly didn't get it.

"Everyone sat and sat and sat," Holly began. "And lots of men stood up and talked. And then for a while no one talked at all. And then we sang. But it was a different kind of singing. And then we sat and sat and sat." Holly made an exasperated sigh. "I never sat so long in my whole life."

Lydia and Sarah laughed. "It takes some getting used to," Lydia gently told Holly. "But you did real good today. For your first time too."

Rachel smiled at Lydia, grateful for the encouragement she was giving Holly. Perhaps Rachel had been too critical of this hardworking woman. Clearly, she cared deeply for Holly too.

"And when it was all done, we ate peanut butter and marshmallow sandwiches." Holly smacked her lips. "Yum-yum."

"I thought you'd like those."

Holly looked curiously at her. "How did you know I had peanut butter and marshmallow sandwiches?"

Rachel shrugged as she handed the last pan to Lydia to rinse. "I had a feeling."

"And then we got to play—all the kids got to play in the barn, Aunt Rachel. It was so fun."

Rachel nodded. "Sounds like fun." She squeezed the water out of the dishrag and looked at Lydia. "Are we done with this dishwater now?"

"Yes." Lydia rinsed the last pot. "You can dump it."

Rachel reached into the deep sink to grasp the large plastic dishpan, lifting the heavy tub and thinking she was going to pour the dishwater down the drain. She had it about chest level when the greasy, soapy plastic edge slipped in her hands and the whole mess tipped toward her and poured right down her front, soaking her sweater and jeans with nasty, greasy, gray soapy dishwater. She let out a shriek and stepped back, but it was too late. Whatever didn't soak her wound up all over the kitchen floor in a slippery, grimy gray puddle. "I'm sorry," she gasped, seeing Lydia's sickened look. "I can clean that up."

"No." Lydia handed her a dish towel to blot herself with. "You go and change out of those clothes. I will take care of this."

"Poor Aunt Rachel," Holly said with sympathy. "I'll go up with you." Then, taking Rachel's hand as if she were a wounded child, Holly led her up the stairs. Once in the bathroom, Rachel carefully peeled off her soggy, messy clothes, piling them in the corner, and suddenly realized she had just ruined her only pair of jeans.

"Can you take those down to Aunt Lydia?" Rachel asked Holly as she wrapped the sodden bundle in a towel to keep it from getting on Holly. "See if she can wash them for me."

"Okay." Holly nodded.

"And when you come back up, can you bring me my pajamas? They're under my pillow on my bed."

"You're going to bed already?" Holly looked surprised.

Rachel shook her head. "I don't have any other clothes to wear." She pointed to the damp bundle. "Those were my only pants."

"Oh." Holly's eyes grew big.

"So take that to Aunt Lydia, okay?"

"And bring back your pajamas?"

"Yes."

After taking a quick bath and getting into her pajamas and into bed, Rachel opened her e-book and decided to make the most of her "early" bedtime. In a way it was a relief to be up here and away from the curious members of the Miller family. She knew she was the misfit in this house. Even Holly, who was just a child, had managed to meld almost seamlessly into the Amish way of life.

Tomorrow, Rachel decided, she would put on her clean clothes and pack her bags, and even if Lydia refused to hand over Holly, Rachel would go and get herself a room in the hotel in town. At least that would give her a place to figure things out. If there was any way to figure this out. Mostly, she wanted to get away from here. The sooner the better. In the meantime, she would enjoy this brief break up here in Sarah's room.

"Aunt Rachel," Holly said as she returned to the room, "you don't have to go to bed now."

Rachel smiled at her. "It's okay. I think this is my punishment for making a mess in the kitchen. An early bedtime." She held up her e-reader. "Besides, I can catch up on my reading. So, really, it's all right."

"But Aunt Lydia found some clothes for you to wear," Holly explained as she played with Rachel's hair.

Sarah came in carrying a bundle of what looked suspiciously like Amish clothing. "Mamm said to give you these," she said quietly.

"Oh, Sarah, that's okay," Rachel told her. "I don't need to wear your mother's clothes. Besides, they'd be too big for me."

"They're not Mamm's clothes," Sarah said. "Noah went over to Mammi's to get them. They used to belong to Aunt Miriam."

"Miri?" Rachel reached over to touch the blue dress.

"Mamm says you are about the same size."

Rachel nodded. "Miri and I used to swap clothes sometimes."

"This was my mommy's?" Holly said as the realization sank in. "When she was Amish?"

"Mamm told me that Mammi saved them," Sarah confided to Holly. "She thought Aunt Miriam would come home someday."

"Oh." Holly got a very sad look, then turned to Rachel. "Can I get in bed with you, Aunt Rachel?"

"Sure."

Holly snuggled up to Rachel in a way that warmed Rachel's heart and gave her hope.

"I want to sleep with Aunt Rachel tonight," she told Sarah. "If it's okay."

Rachel stroked Holly's hair, which had tumbled out of its bun. "It's okay with me, Holly, but it will be pretty snug in this tiny bed."

"You can have my bed," Sarah offered generously.

"Thank you," Rachel told her.

After a while, Holly seemed to recover from her melancholic moment, but now she looked at Rachel hopefully. "Will you please put on the Amish dress, Aunt Rachel?"

"Right now?"

Holly eagerly agreed. "I want to see how you look."

Rachel sighed. "I don't even know how to do it," she said. "All the pins and everything."

"I'll help you, Aunt Rachel," Sarah said.

Rachel was surprised that she'd called her "aunt." "All right," she agreed. "But it seems silly, since it'll be bedtime in an hour or so anyway."

"Please," Holly begged.

So it was that Rachel allowed both Sarah and Holly to dress her up like an Amish woman. Once she had the dress on—although she knew she must look ridiculous—she had to admit that it wasn't uncomfortable. Plus it fit.

"Let's go downstairs," Holly suggested, "and show Aunt Lydia."

The last thing Rachel wanted to do was parade around in this outfit, but both Holly and Sarah looked so hopeful she couldn't refuse them. However, she was somewhat surprised to find that Benjamin was down in the front room. He was talking to Daniel about Buttercup, and he sounded concerned that she hadn't calved yet.

"I want to give her until midnight," Benjamin was saying. "After that . . . well, she might need some help."

"*Ja.*" Daniel slowly nodded. "We cannot let her go too long. It is one thing to lose the calf, but we do not want to lose the cow."

Benjamin looked up to see them standing at the foot of the stairs, listening to this conversation. "Oh!" He looked surprised. "Rachel, is that you?"

"She's wearing my mother's old Amish clothes," Holly proclaimed.

"I spilled dishwater all over my clothes," Rachel explained quickly.

He nodded with a hard-to-read expression.

"Is Buttercup going to be okay?" Rachel asked.

Benjamin shrugged. "I hope so."

"Who's Buttercup?" Holly asked with concern.

Sarah quickly filled her in and then Holly begged to go out to the barn to see, and Daniel acted like it was perfectly fine.

"Is it really okay?" Rachel asked Benjamin.

"Sure. If she wants to."

"I want to—I want to," Holly said eagerly. "I've never seen a calf being born before."

"I haven't either." Rachel tossed Benjamin a look now. "But I mean is it *okay* . . . as in, well, is Buttercup's calf going to be *okay*?"

Benjamin gave her a look that showed he understood her meaning, then turned to Holly. "Here's the deal, Holly. You can come out to watch for a while, but if I decide that Buttercup doesn't need an audience, you can't complain if I say it's time to come back to the house. Do you understand?"

She nodded somberly. "Yes. You mean if Buttercup is uncomfortable with too many people watching her, right?"

He grinned. "*Ja*. Right."

And so they bundled up, and Holly, Sarah, and Rachel followed Benjamin out to the barn, where they gathered around Buttercup, waiting for her miracle—at least Rachel hoped it would be a miracle—to begin.

9

After more than an hour of waiting for poor Buttercup to calve, watching as the anxious cow lay down, then stood up, again and again, Rachel could tell the girls were getting restless. Holly seemed as interested in the calico barn cat Cookie as she was in seeing a birth. Seated on a straw bale, Holly had turned her full skirt into a snug cat bed, and Cookie was purring contentedly.

Even so, Rachel knew it was getting late and was about to call it a night when Lydia came out to the barn and insisted it was time for the girls to go to bed.

"You both have school tomorrow," she told them sternly.

"*I* have school?" Holly gave Rachel a puzzled look as she gently eased Cookie from her warm, comfy bed. "I thought I was on my Christmas vacation."

"School goes all week here," Lydia quickly explained. "Right up until Christmas. And, *ja*, you will go to school with Sarah and Ezra in the morning."

"We get some days off *after* Christmas," Sarah assured Holly. "And don't worry—we're mostly working on our Christmas play this week."

"You're having a Christmas play at your school too?" Holly's eyes lit up. "Is it *A Christmas Carol*?"

Sarah frowned. "I don't know what it's called."

"I'm sure it's not *A Christmas Carol*," Rachel told Holly.

"Will *I* be in the play?" Holly asked hopefully.

"*Ja*, I think so," Sarah said. "I'm playing the innkeeper's wife, and Ezra is Joseph this year. Maybe you can be an animal. The younger children are mostly animals."

"I want to be a horse," Holly proclaimed.

Sarah looked uncertain. "I don't think we have horses in it."

"Come now, *liebschen*." Lydia wrapped an arm around Holly. "It is time to go to bed."

Holly turned to Rachel. "You can stay here and watch Buttercup have her baby," she said. "You don't have to go to school tomorrow."

"*Ja*," Lydia told her. "You do not need to go inside unless you want to, Rachel. I will see the girls go to bed."

Once again, Rachel felt dismissed, but it seemed pointless to resist. Lydia was clearly in charge of her household. Besides, Rachel was curious to witness a cow giving birth. "All right," she told Holly. "I'll stay here. But first let me kiss you good night." She bent down to hug and kiss Holly. "Good night, sleep tight, and don't let the bedbugs bite."

Holly giggled at the familiar saying, but Lydia gave her a confused frown.

"I don't have bugs in my bed," Sarah told Holly as they headed for the door.

"It's just a joke," Holly said. "My daddy used to say it to me."

The barn grew quiet now, with just the sounds of the animals and Buttercup rustling around, trying to get comfortable. "Do you think she's going to be okay?" Rachel asked Benjamin as she sat back down on the milking stool that he had provided for her.

"I think so. She's never had a problem before, but there's always a first."

"What would you do if she did have a problem?" Rachel wasn't really sure she wanted to hear the answer, and yet she was curious.

"Well, it's not something I want to do, but I would have to sacrifice the calf in order to save the cow, and it wouldn't be pretty. If it comes to that—and it won't be until after midnight—I'll need you to go in and get Daniel to help me. And I'm sure you won't want to watch." He peered at her from over Buttercup's back, from where he was rubbing her side in the hopes the calf would turn around. "You might not want to stay out here that late."

She shrugged. "I don't know. It's not easy sleeping in a strange place, and the cot wasn't too comfy. I'm sure I was wide awake for half the night."

His brows arched.

"I'm sorry, I didn't mean to complain. Your sister is kind to put me up like this." Rachel reached down to where Cookie was rubbing against her legs, and as soon as she petted the cat, she hopped up into Rachel's lap, which Rachel didn't mind a bit, because the warmth was nice.

He grinned. "No problem. You can complain to me. I wouldn't like sleeping on a cot either."

"And I'm sure I've worn out my welcome," she continued. For some reason she felt comfortable letting her guard down around this guy. She knew he was Amish, yet he didn't seem as rigid as Lydia and Daniel.

"Lydia is curious as to why you're still here," he told her.

"Well, for one thing there's the snow," she began. "She seems to think it's no big deal, but that Karmann Ghia is not made for this kind of weather."

"Uh-huh. That's a nice little car."

She frowned. "I just don't get you, Benjamin."

"What do you mean?"

"I mean, you're dressed like them. And I know you're Amish, but for some reason, you seem different."

He pointed at her with a funny grin. "Well, you're dressed Amish, but I have to say you're pretty different too."

"I already told you the reason I'm dressed like this. I am obviously not Amish."

"So clothes don't make the man? Or the woman either?"

"Maybe not, but appearances do seem very important to Amish people, and I have to admit that bewilders me. I mean, from my perspective, it seems a bit superficial." Now she pointed at his face. "Another thing that's different—you don't have one of those weird fringy beards. Why is that?"

"Fringy beards?" He laughed.

"All the men at the church meeting seemed to have them. Why don't you?"

"Because I'm not married," he said simply.

"Oh? So if you get married, you'll have to wear a beard like that?" She scratched the top of the cat's head, making her purr even louder.

"That's what's expected."

"And why aren't you married? You're obviously old enough."

Before he could answer, Buttercup let out a loud bellow and Benjamin was barely able to hop out of the way before she turned herself completely around in the oversized stall and then just as quickly turned back around the other way. "Easy, girl," he said as he moved over to where Rachel and Cookie had evacuated the stool, getting out of the way of the restless bovine.

"Is she okay?"

"She's in pain." He bent down to examine her hindquarters again. Since Buttercup's head was toward Rachel now, she couldn't see what Benjamin saw. "But I think her situation is improving."

"Really?" Rachel looked into Buttercup's big brown eyes. "I'm sorry you're having such a hard time, girl," she said soothingly. "I wish there was something I could do to help." She stepped closer, petting the silky brown neck.

"You can pray that these hooves come out pointing down," he told her.

Buttercup let out another guttural noise, as if she were moaning in pain. Rachel felt so sorry for her that she actually did close her eyes and silently asked God to help this poor animal. Really, what could it hurt?

"I think it's about to happen," Benjamin said eagerly. "I can see the sac."

"What about the hooves?" she asked. "Are they pointing down? I did pray just now."

"I can't tell, but if they're pointing up, you'll have to run for Daniel. And I mean *run*."

Rachel bit her lip, waiting nervously. "Should I run now?"

"No, not yet. I think we might've gotten lucky. Now if she

could just settle down . . . and lie down . . . I think we might be out of the woods."

Again Rachel prayed. She felt a bit silly praying for a cow, but at the same time, it was better than just fretting. Suddenly Buttercup started to move again, turning around once more, and then she lay down. This time her head was faced away from Rachel.

"Thanks be to God," Benjamin came over and, grabbing up the other milking stool, sat right near Buttercup's back end. "It won't be long."

The whole barn seemed quiet now, as if the other animals were aware that something important was going on over here. Or else they were asleep. And then, in a matter of seconds, it happened. The calf's hooves emerged, pointing the right direction, followed by the head, and just like that, the entire calf was out. Between Buttercup and Benjamin, the shiny dark brown calf was getting his nose cleared and cleaned, and after what seemed a long time, but was probably just seconds, he was breathing.

"I wish Holly could see this," Rachel said quietly, watching with wide-eyed amazement.

"Move out of the way," Benjamin said as he lifted the calf in his arms. "I'm taking him over to a clean stall."

"What about his mommy?" Rachel looked at the cow, now resting peacefully.

"Don't worry, she won't be far behind." He walked over to another stall. "Can you get this door for me, Rachel?"

She hurried over, opening the latch and holding the door wide open. Just like Benjamin predicted, Buttercup was on her feet, letting out a protective sounding *moo* and following him into the clean stall.

"There you go, old girl," Benjamin said as he gently laid the calf down, allowing Buttercup to sniff and check him out. "You should both rest comfortably tonight." He stepped out and closed the door, then turned back to Rachel. "Thanks for your help."

She shrugged. "I wasn't much help, but I did enjoy witnessing that, in a weird sort of way. I mean, I'm a city girl, but that was pretty cool. Okay, cool's not the right word. It was amazing—miraculous." She laughed, suddenly feeling giddy with relief. She had really been worried about Buttercup and the calf.

"It is amazing. I'm glad you stuck it out for the whole thing." He picked up some straw, using it to wipe his hands, then tossing it into the stall where the birthing had just occurred. "I need to get this cleaned up now, and I expect you'll want to get back to the house."

She wasn't eager to leave, but at the same time she didn't really want to help clean up the stall, which was a bit smelly. "Thanks for letting me watch," she said.

"Make sure Holly comes out here to see it in the morning," he told her. "The calf will be all dry and soft and fluffy by then. Nothing cuter than a baby calf."

"Holly will probably fall in love with it."

"And I'm sure she'll get the opportunity to see a complete calving," he assured her. "We've got a number of cows due to calve this spring—she won't miss out."

"Yeah . . ." Rachel sighed sadly. "I'm sure she'll enjoy that." She told him good night, and picking up the lantern she'd left hung on the peg by the door, she hurried out and on over to the darkened house.

It felt strange to be out here in the middle of the night, still wearing the Amish dress—a dress that had belonged to Miri. Her footsteps crunched in the snow, and halfway between the barn and the house, she paused to look up at the night sky, wondering if more snow was in store, but all she saw was velvety black and stars. Millions of twinkling stars. She had never seen stars like that before, so bright and so close, almost as if she could touch them with her hand. She just stood there, staring up in wonder, until she realized she was shivering, and then she hurried into the house.

As she carried her lantern through the darkened house, tiptoeing up the stairs, it almost felt like she was having a love-hate relationship with the Amish. At times, like watching the calving tonight, she felt completely alive and engaged and was enjoying herself immensely—and those stars were awesome! Even some of the slowed-down simple pleasures of preparing food or enjoying a sunset over a snowy field were all wonderful. But then there was Lydia—and the way her grasp upon Holly seemed to be growing tighter and tighter while, at the same time, she was pushing Rachel away. That thought caused all of Rachel's good feelings to dissolve, and once again she felt nothing but animosity toward the Amish.

10

The next morning, even before breakfast, Rachel took Holly out to the barn to see the new calf. Thankfully, Sarah was helping her mother with the cooking, and Rachel was able to savor this moment with her niece by herself. As Holly petted the velvety brown calf, Rachel told her the whole dramatic story of how the calf was born.

"You watched the whole thing?" Holly asked with child-like awe.

"Yes, and I sort of helped." She chuckled. "Well, I probably wasn't much help, but Benjamin seemed to appreciate it."

"What's his name?" Holly asked.

"I have no idea."

"I would call him Cocoa," Holly told her. "He's the same color as cocoa."

"Maybe you should tell Uncle Benjamin."

"Yeah." She nodded eagerly. "I will."

After breakfast, Jacob announced that it was time to go to school, and Holly was ecstatic over what was about to be her first buggy ride. Although Rachel was happy for her, it was painful to watch her niece, dressed up in the Amish outfit, climbing into the buggy with Sarah. It all felt so wrong . . . and so final. As if Rachel might never see her again, as if Holly was riding off into Amish Land for good.

Rachel had been forced to wear the Amish clothes too, because at breakfast, she discovered that laundry wasn't usually done until Saturday.

"But I put your clothing in a tub to soak," Lydia said as she scrubbed a plate. "And I will wash them out after I finish in here."

"I can wash my clothes myself," Rachel said.

Lydia looked doubtful. "The way we wash clothes here is not like you are used to. I will do it."

"Then let me finish in the kitchen," Rachel insisted.

Lydia looked even more doubtful. "What if you pour dishwater on yourself again—and all over the floor?"

"I'll be very careful."

Lydia sighed. "*Ja*, I would like to get your clothes washed out so we can hang them to dry. It will take most of the day to dry, and I think you must be wanting to be on your way by now."

Rachel felt the need to bite her tongue as Lydia went out to the back porch, where her laundering area was set up. As badly as Rachel longed to be "on her way," she did not want to leave without Holly—although the likelihood of leaving *with* Holly seemed to be shrinking by the moment. Just the memory of Holly's smiling face as she waved from the buggy as it was leaving made Rachel feel like crying as she washed and rinsed a plate.

She'd just finished washing the last pot when Lydia came

back into the house with Rachel's clean but wet clothes. "I will hang these by the fire," Lydia told her. "That will help them to dry faster."

"Thank you." Rachel cringed to see her red wool sweater all pulled out of shape, but she knew it was pointless to complain. She should simply be grateful. This time, when she emptied the dishpan, she did it very carefully—with no mishaps. Lydia was just returning to the kitchen as Rachel was rinsing it out.

"You have learned how to do it right?"

Rachel sighed. "I guess so."

Lydia picked up a dishrag, wiping over the countertop that Rachel had already cleaned, as if to show that it hadn't been done properly. "Mamm told me you spoke to her yesterday," Lydia said without looking at Rachel, "but that you ran away."

Rachel's cheeks flushed to remember her embarrassing breakdown in front of the older woman. "Yes. I got emotional when we spoke about your sister . . . and my brother. I suppose I'm still grieving."

"*Ja.*" Lydia just nodded. "I understand."

Rachel felt somewhat surprised and was about to pursue this more, but Lydia seemed to change gears. "Mamm wants you to come and see her today," Lydia informed her. "I told her you would come after breakfast."

"Oh?"

"*Ja.* I have my work to do and you cannot leave until your clothes are dry, so you might as well go now." Lydia turned and walked away.

Rachel really felt Lydia's people skills could use some improvement, but the thought of finishing her conversation with Miri's mother—in private—was somewhat appealing. If nothing else, she might discover why Miri had left here. Not that Rachel blamed her. She felt certain she would've done the same thing if she'd been in Miri's shoes. She looked down at her dress, realizing that she was almost in Miri's shoes now. At least Benjamin was correct—these outfits with the thick black stockings and all the undergarments were warmer than they looked.

Even so, she put on her own coat before she headed over to Mrs. Schrock's house, where she was soon seated opposite the older woman at a dining table very much like the one in Lydia's house, having a cup of tea. She apologized immediately for having fallen apart on Sunday. "It's still difficult for me," she said. "My brother and Miri were the only family I have. And Holly too, of course."

"You have no other family?" Mrs. Schrock looked skeptical.

"My father left us when I was very young. We never saw him again, and my mother died when I was fifteen."

"I'm sorry."

"Michael helped take care of me. He was a very fine man." She told about how Michael got scholarships for law school but also managed to provide for her by working part-time jobs. "He paid for me to go through flight attendant school," she continued, "because I wanted to see the world. And that's how I met Miri—I mean Miriam. She came to work for the same airline, and we became friends right away. I knew from the first time I met her that Miri was special."

Mrs. Schrock let out a sad sigh but said nothing.

"At first Miri and I were roommates, but then I introduced her to my brother. It didn't take long before they fell in love.

118

Miri kept working for the airline, but then she got pregnant with Holly. She wasn't exactly happy to be pregnant."

"She was not happy?" Mrs. Schrock looked surprised as she set down her cup.

"She didn't want to give up her job."

"Oh."

"And she worked for a while, but eventually she decided to be a full-time mom." Rachel paused, wondering if she was talking too fast. Was Mrs. Schrock really getting all this? "Michael and Miri and Holly were all the family I had," she said again, hoping that this woman might have a heart underneath her severe black dress. "Do you know how lucky you are to have so much family around you?"

She made a sad smile. "*Ja*. I am blessed."

"Having Lydia and her family right next door must be so nice for you," Rachel continued. "And then you have Benjamin and your other daughter not too far away. Does she have children too?"

"*Ja*. Ruth has five children."

"Wow. You have ten grandchildren. You are lucky."

"*Ja*. I am blessed. I hope to have great-grandchildren too. I expect Jacob will marry soon, and he and his new wife will come live here and work my farm."

"I thought Benjamin worked this farm."

She shrugged. "*Ja* . . . we will see."

Rachel felt confused but was determined not to get distracted. She was on a mission now. Somehow she had to make this old woman, who appeared to be the matriarch of this family, realize how vital it was for Rachel to take Holly home with her. "So you have ten grandchildren," Rachel continued.

"And you will have even more great-grandchildren before long, but all I have is Holly." She sighed. "And now I am losing her."

Mrs. Schrock nodded with a sympathetic expression. "*Ja*. I am sorry for your loss, Rachel. But you are a young woman. You will marry and have children of your own."

"I'm not that young," Rachel insisted. "I turn thirty-five this week."

Mrs. Schrock blinked. "That old?"

Of course, this didn't make Rachel feel any better. "Yes. That old. And I'm not even married. My chances of having children get smaller all the time, but Holly is like a daughter to me and I really believe she belongs—"

"I know where you are going, but I have a question for you."

"What?"

"If all you say is true—why did your brother and my daughter leave Holly to Lydia in their will?"

Rachel took in a quick breath and then spilled out the story of Curtis Garman. Oh, she didn't go into all the details, but enough to show that she was estranged from Michael and Miri for a while. "But when I realized they were right, Holly was just turning one, and everything between Michael and Miri and me was smoothed out. They even made me Holly's godmother."

"Godmother?" She frowned. "What is that?"

"It means I am supposed to help Holly grow up into a strong Christian woman."

"Oh? And how would you do that?"

"I have already been taking her to church and—"

"But that is not the kind of church she needs." Mrs. Schrock peered intensely at Rachel. "And living with a single woman who flies around in airplanes is not a good way for a little girl to be raised. Can you see that?"

"But I gave up my job to take care of Holly."

"You told me what it was like for you, Rachel, growing up with only a mother to provide for you, and then she died. It was very hard. You had no family. What if that happens to Holly? What if you were alone, with no family, and you died? What would become of Holly?"

"But I—"

"*Hear me.* Do you wish upon Holly what you had? Or do you love her enough to give her your blessing and allow her to remain here with her family? Can you not see that Almighty God has returned Holly to us? That he has brought her here for a reason? Do you want to be selfish? Do you only want your way? Or can you trust God?"

Once again, tears filled Rachel's eyes. "I . . . I don't know. Maybe you're right. Maybe I am selfish when it comes to Holly, but I love her, Mrs. Schrock. I truly love her. But, it's true, I need her too."

"What does Holly need?"

Rachel nodded, slowly standing. "I see your point." She blinked, trying not to cry in front of her again. "Thank you for your time. If you will excuse me."

"Sometimes it is the hard things that are the best," she said as Rachel pulled on her coat. "The gem cannot be polished without friction."

"Good-bye, Mrs. Schrock," Rachel called as she headed for the front door. "Thank you for your hospitality."

After she got outside in the cold winter air, she allowed the tears to flow freely. She knew Mrs. Schrock was right.

121

Rachel was being selfish. Entirely selfish. It was plain to see that Holly loved it here. What child wouldn't? Rachel herself would've loved to have grown up here as a child. To have all this, horse-and-buggy rides, calves being born, and a big family too? Who was she kidding? It was a dream come true.

Rachel's plan now was to wait until Holly came home from school and then explain the entire situation to her. So far she had not been completely honest with her niece. It was time that Holly understood the conditions of her parents' will. Then, after she felt assured that Holly was okay and that she was happy about remaining with her new family, Rachel would drive the car into town and spend the night at the hotel. After that . . . well, it wasn't a complete plan, but at least it was a plan.

No one seemed to be around as she entered the house, and so she used this opportunity to slip upstairs unnoticed, going into Sarah's room and closing the door. To pass the time until Holly came home, she would read and nap. She hoped no one would come looking for her. Really, why should Lydia care whether she came down for lunch or not? Her stomach was so twisted into knots, she knew she couldn't eat anyway. The sooner she handled this and was out of their lives, the better it would be for everyone. Especially Holly.

It was close to three when Rachel discovered her clothes were dry. Or nearly. The jeans still felt slightly damp, but she didn't care. And the sweater would dry later. She'd already packed her overnight bag, and after she was dressed in her own clothing, she neatly folded the Amish clothes, setting them on the end of Sarah's bed. She looked out the window, hoping to see the carriage coming home. How long did these children stay in school anyway?

She went downstairs now, peering out the front window.

"The children will be home soon," Lydia told her with an impatient edge to her voice. "They always get home about now, and then they do chores."

"It's just that I wanted to speak to Holly," Rachel told her. "To tell her good-bye."

Lydia's eyes brightened with interest. "Are you leaving? Going home?"

"Yes." Rachel studied her. They might've been friends if they'd met under different circumstances. "But I want to talk to Holly first."

"*Ja*. That is good. I know she will miss you, Rachel. I can see you are close."

"We are," Rachel agreed.

Lydia smiled, and for a moment, Rachel thought she could see Miri in her. "Please, know that you are welcome to visit us, Rachel, anytime you like. Our door is always open to you."

Rachel felt that familiar lump in her throat, but she was not giving in to it. "Thank you. I appreciate that." Just then a buggy appeared on the road. "Is that them?"

"*Ja*." Lydia nodded.

Rachel got her coat and pulled it on, going outside to meet them over by the barn. "Hi, darling," she said as she helped Holly down from the buggy. She hugged her tightly. "Did you have a good day at school?"

Holly shrugged in a tired way. "I guess so."

"Are you feeling okay?" Rachel touched her forehead, but it seemed fine. Maybe she was hungry and worn out. "I think

Lydia made cookies this morning," she said as they went into the house. "You interested?"

Holly smiled as she peeled off her cloak.

"How about if I get them and we'll sneak them up to Sarah's room."

Holly's brow creased. "Will we get in trouble?"

"This time it's okay. And I need to talk to you. Alone."

"Okay." Holly nodded eagerly, as if she was enjoying this game.

"You go on up there and I'll join you." Rachel went into the kitchen, ready to defend herself for swiping some cookies and a glass of milk for Holly, but thankfully, Lydia wasn't around. She hurried and grabbed the contraband, then slipped upstairs. "Here you go."

Holly took a big bite of a sugar cookie and grinned. "Thanks."

Rachel sat down on the cot, taking in a steadying breath, and then she began. "There's something I need to tell you about your mommy and daddy." She took a moment to explain what a will was and then she told Holly about the first year of Holly's life and how Rachel and Holly's parents hadn't been speaking.

"Mommy and Daddy were mad at you?" Holly looked incredulous.

"We were all acting a little silly, but the good news is that we got over it. In fact, we were all best friends again by your first birthday."

Holly smiled with relief. "I don't remember that birthday."

"No, you wouldn't." Now Rachel explained how Michael had made his will during that first year, when everyone wasn't getting along. "And your daddy put something in the will about you, Holly."

"What?" she asked with wide eyes.

"Your mommy and daddy decided that if anything happened to them, if they both died, you would be sent to Aunt Lydia to live."

"With you too?"

"No. Not with me too. You would live here by yourself. With all your cousins and Aunt Lydia and Uncle Daniel and Uncle Benjamin and your grandma. But I will go back to Chicago to live."

"Without me?"

She nodded. "These people aren't my family, Holly. They are your relatives. You are really lucky to have so many relatives. Did you know that you have five more cousins besides the ones here?"

"No."

"And you've got your new school and the farm and the animals and the horses and—"

"But what about you?" Holly set the cookie back on the plate that was on the dresser.

"What about me?" Rachel forced a smile. "Well, I'm still your aunt, and I'll come to see you whenever I can. And maybe Aunt Lydia will let you come and see me."

"No!" Holly folded her arms across her front.

"No, to what?"

"You can't do this, Aunt Rachel."

Rachel bent down to hug her now. "Holly, I don't want to do this, but it's the way your daddy wrote the will . . . back when we were all mad at each other. And I think he forgot to change it after we were all friends. Or maybe . . . maybe he knew this was a good place for you. And it is, isn't it?" She held Holly back, looking in her face. "Haven't you been happy here?"

"But you were here too."

"I know."

Holly spotted Rachel's packed bag now. "Are you leaving today?"

"I think it might be best."

"No!" Holly stomped her foot this time.

"But I have to go, Holly. There's no place for me here. This is your family, not mine."

"You're my family," Holly insisted. "You told me we were a family, Aunt Rachel. You said you and me would always be together. Remember? After Mommy and Daddy died, you promised."

"I know, but I didn't know about the will, and a will is like the law, Holly. It's something I can't change."

"Then ask Aunt Lydia," Holly pressed. "Tell her that I need to be with you. Tell her we'll come here to visit. I need to go home with you." Her lip quivered. "I miss my room."

Sarah came into the room. "Oh, there you are." She spied the cookies and shook her head. "You can't eat in the bedroom, Holly. You know that." She picked them up.

"Aunt Rachel is leaving!" Holly said angrily.

Sarah looked slightly alarmed too. "What about her birthday tomorrow?"

"That's *right*." Holly turned back to Rachel. "Sarah and I were planning a birthday party—just for you, Aunt Rachel. You can't leave until we have that."

126

Rachel took in a long breath. "Oh, Holly."

"Please, Aunt Rachel. You have to have your birthday party."

"If I stay for my birthday party, will you try to be very brave when it's time for me to go? Because you know I need to go."

Holly looked torn, but she agreed.

"Now we have to go do chores," Sarah told Holly. "And no more food in the bedroom," she said firmly, shaking a finger at her. "After Rachel goes, you will have to start obeying all the rules. Mamm said so."

Rachel felt a shiver of worry run through her, but she knew there was nothing to be done. Her hands were tied. It was inevitable that life would change for Holly. She wouldn't be allowed to keep her dolls and toys and clothes. Her hair would grow long. But those were small things. In the long run she would be okay with it. The Amish might be difficult to understand, but one thing seemed clear—they loved their children, and their children seemed happy. If they ever weren't happy, they could do what Miri had done after she grew up. They could leave. If Holly ever needed to leave, Rachel would be there waiting—ready to greet her with open arms.

11

"I thought you were leaving after you spoke to Holly," Lydia said after Rachel offered to help her with supper. "You might not make it far before dark, but you could get started. And the weather is good and the roads are clear."

"I'm sorry, but you'll have to put up with me for one more night if you don't mind." Rachel explained about the girls' plans to have a birthday party tomorrow. "But I promise to leave as soon as they're done, and Holly understands this."

"Oh?" She blinked. "Sarah did not tell me about a birthday party."

Rachel just shrugged as she reached for the dishes to set the table. "She didn't tell me either. Neither did Holly. I think it was supposed to be a surprise. I doubt it will be much of a party. Don't worry."

The table seemed quieter than usual, and Rachel could tell that Holly was still out of sorts. After dinner, Holly barely said a word as they helped in the kitchen. If Rachel didn't know better, she would suspect Holly was getting sick.

"Will you read to me?" Holly asked her when they were done.

"Sure." Rachel nodded eagerly. "I'd like to."

"Can we read in Sarah's room?" Holly asked Lydia.

"*Ja*. It is all right. This time."

Holly took Rachel's hand and they went upstairs together. "Sarah said that Aunt Lydia likes children to read downstairs after supper, because it's family time."

"Oh," Rachel said.

Up in Sarah's room, Holly started to gather up her toys, packing them into the various bags she'd brought them in.

"What are you doing?" Rachel asked suspiciously. Did Holly think she was going to be able to slip away with her, like thieves in the night?

"I want to send my toys home with you," Holly explained. "Sarah said I can't have them here, and if you don't take them with you, Aunt Lydia will just throw them away."

"Oh." Rachel nodded. "Okay, I can take them."

Holly picked up Bunny and looked into his face. "I'll miss you," she whispered. "But you'll be safe at home."

Rachel wondered how much of this she could possibly take. Eventually, everything, including Bunny and Ivy, were carefully packed and Rachel promised to deliver them to Holly's room, where they could have a happy reunion with the other toys. What would happen to Holly's things on down the line remained to be seen, but it wasn't a question Rachel needed to answer today.

Rachel couldn't remember a more miserable birthday. If not for her promise to Holly, she would've much preferred to be on her way by now. Still, a promise was a promise, and every moment she had left with Holly seemed precious. To pass the time, she helped Lydia with various chores and packed the car and even wandered out to the barn to pay her respects to Buttercup and her calf.

"Hello," Benjamin called out as she came into the barn.

She greeted him back, then asked why he was over here.

"Just checking on the new mom," he told her. "I wanted to see if she was ready to go home yet."

"Go home?"

"*Ja.* Buttercup actually lives next door. She's Mamm's cow. I only brought her over here on Saturday night because I knew she was close to calving and our barn was scheduled for church the next day. I didn't want her to interrupt their service, and I didn't want to leave her outside in the bad weather. Daniel said it was fine for her to calve here."

"Oh, I get it." She reached over to pet the calf. "Well, I came out here to say good-bye to Buttercup and her baby."

"Cocoa," Benjamin supplied.

"Then Holly got her wish." She smiled sadly.

"How did you know they were leaving?"

"What?" She turned to look at him.

"You said you came out here to tell them good-bye."

"Oh." She nodded. "Well, that's because *I'm* leaving."

"Really?" His brow creased. "So soon? What about your birthday party?" Now he put his hand over his mouth. "Oops. I wasn't supposed to let the cat out of the bag."

"It's okay. That cat's long gone now. I promised Holly I wouldn't go until after the party."

"I see." He gave her a half smile. "Well, then, happy birthday."

131

"Thanks." She turned away, suddenly feeling close to tears again. Why couldn't she be stronger?

"Are you going to be okay?"

"Okay?" she asked in a squeaky voice. "Sure. Why not?"

He put a hand on her shoulder. "I mean leaving Holly behind. I know it's not easy, but are you going to be okay?"

Without looking at him, she shrugged. "Sure. I'll be fine."

"I know how you had hoped this would go differently, Rachel. I've seen you with Holly, and I can tell what you have with her is really special. I'm surprised you're just leaving . . . like this. Are you really okay?"

She turned to look at him with tear-filled eyes. "Let's just say I've had better birthdays, okay? And leave it at that." She turned away and hurried out of the barn.

Rachel's afternoon cry probably helped her with keeping up a brave front for her birthday party. By the time Holly led her downstairs to the dining room table, which Sarah and she had decorated with some paper flowers they'd painstakingly made and a few other things, Rachel felt stronger. She was slightly surprised that both Benjamin and his mother were there, but she tried to take everything in stride as they all pretended to be happy eating the lopsided cake that Sarah and Holly had baked last night. Finally, the simple party came to an end and Rachel thanked everyone and announced it was time for her to go. She could see the gratefulness in Lydia's eyes, and she felt relieved too.

"I want to walk you out to the car," Holly told her. "And I'll give you my present out there. Okay?"

"Okay." Rachel took her hand and gave it a squeeze. "That was a lovely party. Thanks."

Once they were outside, Holly produced a small, roughly wrapped package. "Here you go."

Rachel slowly opened it and was surprised and slightly hurt to find the silver locket she'd given Holly on her sixth birthday inside. "You don't want this anymore?"

Holly's eyes were filled with tears. "Sarah said we can't wear jewelry here, Aunt Rachel. It's not allowed. So I want you to have it."

Rachel knelt down and gathered Holly in her arms. "I will keep it safe for you. *Always.*" She was fighting to hold back tears. "And I will love you always, Holly. If you ever need anything, you just call me. You understand?"

"But there's no phone here, remember?"

"Uncle Benjamin has a phone. Out in the barn."

"Oh."

"And you know my cell phone number, don't you?"

Holly recited the number and Rachel kissed her. Worried she wouldn't be able to keep up this strong front for one more minute, she told Holly she had to go. She waved and blew kisses and slowly drove away, careful lest she drive off the road with her vision blurred by her tears.

12

Rachel only made it to the nearby town on the first leg of her journey, yet it felt like a world away—as if she'd traveled through time. She checked into the small hotel, marveling at the modern conveniences like light switches and a thermostat control, and then fell into bed and cried herself to sleep. The next morning she felt stronger and slightly better and even turned on the TV long enough to hear the local news, which was relatively uneventful. Then, after breakfast at Cathy's Café, she was just getting ready to leave for Chicago when her cell phone rang. The number looked unfamiliar, but she answered it quickly.

"Rachel?"

"Yes? Who is this?"

"It's Benjamin Schrock."

"Oh. Hello, Benjamin. How are you?"

"I'm fine, but Holly isn't doing too well."

"Holly?" Panic rushed through her. "What's wrong with Holly?"

"She fell apart after you left yesterday."

"Oh no. Poor Holly."

"I know. Lydia thought she would settle back down after a good night's sleep, but Holly was still just as upset this morning. She refused to get dressed or go to school."

"Oh dear." Rachel's heart twisted with guilt and grief. "This is all my fault."

"Your fault? Why?"

"Oh, it's a long story, but if I'd handled my life differently seven years ago, none of this would be happening now."

"We all have regrets, Rachel."

"I know, and that doesn't help Holly. But why are you calling me? What can I do about this?"

"Holly is begging for you to come back."

"Come back?" Rachel closed her eyes and took in a deep breath. As badly as she wanted to see Holly, she did not want to return to the Miller farm. It was just too hard.

"Yes. Holly begged Lydia to let you come back long enough to be here for her birthday and Christmas. I think that might help her to make this transition."

"Maybe . . . but Lydia doesn't want me there, Benjamin. She's made it obvious." Rachel looked across the street at the hotel. "Although, I could just stay here in town. Then I could come out and visit Holly after school, spend some time with her each day until Christmas. Do you think that would work? To help Holly adjust?"

"I think that sounds like a very good plan. And very generous on your part, Rachel."

"Or selfish. I'll bet your mother would call it selfish." She instantly regretted this comment. "And maybe she's right."

Fortunately, he just laughed. "*Ja.* That sounds like Mamm."

Suddenly she was curious about him again. How did he really fit in there? He looked Amish, but he never really sounded or acted particularly Amish. How was that okay with his family? Perhaps if she was going to be around a few more days, she would find out more about him.

"So what should I do now?" she asked. "Come back and spend the whole day with Holly? Or will that just aggravate Lydia?"

"I have an idea. How about if I go tell Holly that if she lets me take her to school, you will be at the house by the time she gets home? That way Lydia can't hold it against you."

"Thank you. That sounds perfect."

"See you later, then?"

"Yes," she told him. "I would like to see you later."

"Really?" He sounded surprisingly hopeful.

"Yes. I have a feeling you can shed some light on the Amish thing, Benjamin. That is, if you're willing to talk openly. There's a whole lot that I don't understand about your people."

"You're in good company."

Again, he was being so cryptic and mysterious. Would she ever get him to open up? "There are questions I have about Miri too," she continued. "Why she left and all that. Would you be willing to fill me in?"

"Happy to. Do you have any plans for lunch?"

"For lunch?"

"*Ja.* I thought I could come into town after I drop Holly at school. I have some errands to run anyway."

So it was agreed they would meet for lunch at the same café where she'd just had breakfast. In the meantime, she had some of her own errands to run. If she was going to stick around until Christmas, she would need more than one pair of jeans to wear, and it wouldn't hurt to have a sturdier pair of boots. On her way out of the café, she asked the waitress if there was a place to shop for clothes in town. "The only place is Anne Marie's, just two blocks down," she told her. "But don't expect much."

After shopping about an hour, Rachel thought the waitress's warning was warranted, but she did manage to find a few pieces to extend her very minimalist wardrobe. She wasn't sure if it was the Amish influence or the limited selection, but everything she picked out was relatively plain and simple. From the black sweater to the gray trousers. Even the dress, which she forced herself to buy out of respect for their culture, was a somber green color, but at least the cut was flattering. Then she went across the street and found a pair of lace-up boots that looked as if they'd stand up to some snow.

Then she returned to the hotel, checked herself back in, and proceeded to unload her car for the second time in less than twenty-four hours. She returned to Cathy's Café to wait for Benjamin. For some reason she was surprised to see him arriving in the horse-drawn buggy, which he parked in front. It was as if she'd forgotten he was Amish.

She waved to him, and he came in and made himself comfortable in the booth, removing his dark broad-brimmed hat and setting it on the seat beside him. "Holly is happily in school," he informed her. "Greatly relieved to know that you're not really gone."

"Thank you." She smiled.

After they ordered, she jumped right in. "Excuse me for not beating around the bush, but why did Miri leave?"

"Do you want my opinion or would you like Lydia's version?"

She considered this. "I'll go with your opinion."

"She didn't belong there."

"That's it?"

He shrugged. "Miriam had always dreamed of bigger things. She had wanted to travel and see how the rest of the world lived. So did I."

She blinked. "You wanted to leave too?"

He nodded.

"But you didn't."

"See, that's where you'd be wrong."

"You left?"

"*Ja.* I left shortly after Miriam did. I'd actually hoped to find her and make sure she was okay, but she didn't leave much of a trail."

"When I first met her she called herself Miri Smith," Rachel told him.

"And I was looking for Miriam Schrock. Anyway, I figured she'd make it. She was always smart and motivated."

"So you went back home then?"

"No. I didn't go home until last spring when my father died. Oh, I stayed in touch with my family, because I knew how badly it had hurt them when Miriam left without ever looking back. So I would write them regularly and visit sometimes. Then, when my father died . . . well, I knew my mother was having a hard time. She'd lost Miriam and Daed and she'd sort of lost me. I felt like I owed her something."

"So, tell me, are you Amish or not?"

"It depends on how you define it. I grew up Amish, but I never got baptized. To an outsider I'm Amish. To real Amish, I'm not."

"Oh . . . and is that okay with you?"

"Sure. I know who I am, and as much as I love some of the Amish ways, I know that I don't have it in me to live how they live."

"Why not?"

"Would you be able to do it?"

She considered this as the waitress put a bowl of soup in front of her and a burger in front of Benjamin. Could she do it? Would she do it? "You know . . ." she began slowly after the waitress left, "I almost think I could do it . . . for Holly."

"Really? You would change your religion and your entire culture and your way of life to be near Holly?"

She nodded. "Yes. I think I would." Now she felt hopeful. "Would they let me?"

"You can't be serious."

"I am serious. I can't believe I didn't think of this before."

"But, Rachel, you have no idea what you're saying."

"I like a lot of the things about the Amish," she protested.

"*Ja.* So do I, but there are a lot of things you wouldn't like. Trust me. I know what I'm talking about. Why do you think Miriam left?"

"You said it was because she wanted to travel."

"That was only partly true. She couldn't stand the restrictions of the Ordnung."

"What's that?"

"A book of rules basically. It covers everything from the color you can paint your buggy, to what kind of suspenders you must wear, to demanding you have no wires running from your house to the outside world. Very restrictive."

"Why?"

"I'll give you the nutshell answer. The Amish believe that if they hold fast to the old ways, it will set them apart and keep them humble and help them to maintain their families, and most of all to please God. I could give you a much more complex answer, but that's the gist of it."

"And you really think I wouldn't fit in there?"

He looked at her for a long moment. "I think you've got too much spirit. I wouldn't want to see you change yourself to fit in."

"Not even for Holly?"

Now he looked torn. "I guess I have no right to answer that for you."

"Do you think there's a chance they could ever accept me if I did become Amish? I mean even if it was for Holly's sake?"

"They would expect you to convert to the faith and be baptized for God's sake, not Holly's. You'd have to convince them you were sincere. It's not like a club where you say you want in and they hand you a membership card."

"Can people marry in?"

He laughed. "No."

"I didn't mean *you*," she clarified. "Besides, you admitted you weren't really Amish." However, if he *were* truly Amish and interested in her, she would most certainly consider it.

"Well, you *could* marry an Amishman, and I'm sure there would be some who might be interested, but you would still have to convert to the faith and convince them you were doing it sincerely."

"Oh."

"Come on, Rachel, you wouldn't really do that."

"No . . . I'm just desperate."

They talked some more and she discovered that he'd traveled as much as she had, although he'd actually lived in some of the countries she'd only visited. She also learned that he'd owned several businesses but had sold the last one before coming home to help his mother.

"So what's next for you?" she asked as they were finishing up. "Will you remain in Amish country indefinitely?"

"I have to admit that I'm enjoying the farm and seeing my family, but unless I get baptized, which I don't plan on doing, Mamm will be handing the farm on to her grandsons. Probably Jacob or Noah, especially since they've both been baptized. And that's fine by me. Amishmen have a hard time starting out. There's only so much land." He sighed. "My parents divided their property when I was eighteen. Their plan was for me to have the farm that Lydia and Daniel have now."

"You didn't want it?"

"Sure, I wanted it. I just didn't want to be baptized. I didn't want to be controlled by their beliefs."

"So do you believe in God?"

He laughed. "Of course. I'm fine with God and the Bible. I just don't believe in the Ordnung."

"So what would you do if your mother gave the farm to your nephews?"

He scratched his head. "Maybe I'd go buy myself another farm—but not in an Amish settlement. Maybe somewhere around here. This is some pretty good farmland. I know of a couple properties that are for sale, but it's a big decision."

"At least you'd still have your family nearby."

"*Ja.*" He slowly nodded.

Finally, Rachel thanked him for helping with Holly and for meeting her like this. "It's really helped me to understand some things," she said.

"I just hope it hasn't put any crazy ideas into your head about becoming Amish."

She sighed. "I know it's probably impossible, but I guess I just don't know what else to do."

"Some English have tried it, but very few succeed. If you didn't grow up Amish, it's pretty hard to adapt."

"Do you think Holly will adapt?"

He shrugged. "As I was taking her to school she was complaining about not having a Christmas tree."

"Amish don't believe in Christmas trees?"

"Nope."

"Oh. But you do celebrate Christmas, don't you? The children are putting on the nativity play."

"Yes, but an Amish Christmas is very plain and simple. Family and food and a few gifts. Nothing like an English Christmas."

"I'm not particularly fond of all that goes with Christmas anyway. It's all pretty commercial and frantic and crazy. I think the English, as you call them, could use a little more 'plain and simple' in their Christmas traditions. Although I do think a Christmas tree is nice."

He smiled. "Me too." He looked at the clock above the counter. "I should get back. This is the slow time of year, but there's still lots to be done."

"What about your errands?"

He looked sheepish as he reached for the bill and his hat. "I think I took care of the most important errand."

She thanked him, walking to the register, where he got in line behind another customer. "I guess I'll be seeing you around," she said.

"I sure hope so." He tipped his hat, and as she left, she felt a warm rush. Was it possible he felt it too? she wondered.

Feeling inexplicably merry, she now decided to do some more shopping. If she was spending Christmas with the Millers, she would need to have some presents—some very simple presents—to give to all of them. Presents that would be from both her and Holly. She would buy them and Holly could wrap them. Where they would put them remained to be seen.

13

Rachel planned to arrive at the Millers' about the same time the buggy would come home from school, but seeing she was early, she decided to just remain in the car. It seemed easier that way. However, she noticed Lydia peeking out the window at her.

Then when the buggy arrived, she got out and went to meet Holly, who had leaped from the barely stopped carriage. "Aunt Rachel! Aunt Rachel!" she cried as if she hadn't seen her in weeks. They hugged and Holly went limp in her arms. "Please, don't leave me again."

Rachel explained the plan to remain at the hotel for a while. "I'll sleep there, since Aunt Lydia's house is a little crowded, but I'll be here every day when you come home from school."

"And you'll stay until bedtime?" Holly asked as they went inside. "And read me a story and tuck me in and kiss me good night?"

"I will tonight," she promised. After that, they would have to see. Holly didn't need to know all the details.

Supper was a bit stiff and quiet, and Rachel knew it was

because of her. She was sure the whole family would've been happier to have known she was in Chicago by now. As usual, she helped to clean up afterward, but Lydia seemed even more tight-lipped now. After they finished, Rachel felt somewhat encouraged to see that Holly was warming up to Daniel. She even sat on his lap and laughed when he tickled her. It was reassuring to see her having some good rapport with the man who would become her father figure.

Eventually it was bedtime and Rachel fulfilled her promise by helping Holly with her bedtime routine, but she sensed that Sarah didn't appreciate the intrusion.

"You know, Sarah can read to you when I'm not here," Rachel reminded Holly. "I heard her. She's a good reader."

"*Ja,*" Sarah agreed. "I like reading your bedtime story-book, Holly."

"I know, but Aunt Rachel does it really good." Holly tightened her grasp on Rachel's hand, tugging her toward the bed. "And Aunt Rachel knows how to tuck me in just right."

Finally, it was time for the last good-night kiss. Rachel knew that Holly had dragged out her bedtime rituals long enough that it was only a matter of minutes before Lydia would pop in and put a frosty end to the aunt-and-niece lovefest. "I'll see you tomorrow after school." Rachel picked up the lantern. "I hope you have a good day at school, Holly. Then the next day will be your birthday."

Rachel was relieved to see that it was a clear night as she drove to town. She thought she'd heard something in the forecast about another storm coming, but she hadn't really paid attention. She hoped the fair weather would hold until after Christmas.

Thursday went much as the previous day with Rachel meeting Holly after school, but instead of staying around until bedtime, Rachel excused herself earlier. "I have some things to do," she whispered to Holly, "to get ready for a little event that is coming tomorrow."

"You mean my birthday?" Holly's eyes lit up.

Rachel gave her a mysterious smile. "Maybe."

"Okay." Holly nodded. "I guess you can go."

Relieved to get away without tears or a scene, Rachel kissed Holly good night and promised to return with some surprises for tomorrow. Her plan was to spend the early part of Friday trying to get something special together for Holly's birthday. However, she knew she couldn't make it too special. Lydia would frown on that, and that wouldn't help with Holly's transition from English to Amish.

The next day as Rachel was making her rounds in the small town, she decided to splurge on a chocolate birthday cake. She knew she should've coordinated this with Lydia, but she also knew the Amish enjoyed their sweets. A chocolate cake would probably not go to waste. She also got colorful plates and napkins and balloons and crepe paper as well as some party games. She knew these bright things would look foreign in the stark Miller house, but they could be quickly disposed of afterward.

Finding an appropriate birthday present was more of a challenge. Finally she decided on an art set and tablet. Simple, yes, but hopefully it wouldn't get taken away, and she knew her creative niece could put it to good use. Rachel decided to go a couple hours early in order to set up the birthday party, and to her relief, Lydia wasn't in the house. Feeling a bit intrusive, but not really caring, she let herself in, and relieved that the midday meal was cleaned up, she began setting up the party, transforming the dining table into a bright, festive place.

"What are you doing?" Lydia demanded when she showed up a little before three.

"Hello." Rachel forced a smile. "I'm setting up Holly's party."

Lydia frowned. "This is too much."

Rachel shrugged. "Yes. I probably went overboard, but since it's the last chance I'll get—"

"And a cake?" Lydia pointed at the bakery cake with a personalized greeting piped on. "I already made a cake."

"Then we'll have two cakes." Rachel's smile tightened.

"Two cakes?" Lydia shook her head.

"I'm sure it will be nice to have some extra cake for tomorrow. For Christmas."

Lydia made an exasperated sigh and walked away. Feeling a tiny victory, Rachel continued blowing up balloons. Was she doing this for herself or for Holly? Maybe it didn't matter. Mostly she hoped that everyone would have a good time. For Holly's sake.

As with Rachel's party, Benjamin and Mrs. Schrock came, along with the rest of the family, but thanks to Lydia's sour disposition, which had not improved, there seemed to be a damper on the festivities. Eventually even Rachel's enthusiasm diminished, although she tried to hide it.

"Time to blow out your candles," Rachel told Holly.

"I'm going to make a wish," Holly proclaimed. She closed her eyes and got a very intense expression. Rachel glanced across the table to see that Benjamin was looking directly at her, and when their eyes met, she felt a rush of warmth. Holly blew out all the candles, except for one that remained lit, and she turned to Rachel with troubled eyes. "My wish!"

"It's okay," Rachel assured her. "Just blow it out."

Holly blew it out, then shook her head. "It won't work now."

"What did you wish for?" Sarah asked curiously.

Holly looked at Rachel, then frowned. "I'm not going to get it, am I?"

"Time to cut the cake," Rachel said cheerfully. "It's your favorite, Holly. Chocolate." As she served cake and ice cream, she tried to keep the atmosphere jovial, but it was an uphill battle. The older boys were polite but quiet, and the adults seemed clueless as to how to make a child's birthday party much fun. Or else they just didn't like Rachel. She suspected that was the real problem. Finally, Lydia made it clear that the party was over and it was time to attend to chores.

"I hope you had fun," Rachel told Holly as they cleaned up the colorful debris.

"Can I keep the balloons and streamers?" Holly asked hopefully.

"I guess so. Unless Aunt Lydia doesn't want you to."

"I'll put them in Sarah's room," Holly said, gathering them up.

When she came back downstairs, Rachel was just shoving a big wad of paper plates, napkins, and tablecloth into the woodstove, where it quickly *whooshed* into flames and disappeared up the chimney.

Holly let out a sad little sigh.

"Are you okay, sweetie?" Rachel kneeled down and looked into her eyes.

Holly just shook her head, and Rachel could tell by the quivering chin, she was close to tears. "My birthday wish was to go home with you, Aunt Rachel."

She nodded. "I thought so." To distract Holly, Rachel told her about the Christmas presents she'd gotten for the Miller family. "They'll be from you and me, but I thought maybe you could wrap them."

"All by myself?"

"Do you mind?"

She smiled. "I like wrapping presents."

"They're in the car," Rachel told her. "Along with some wrapping paper and ribbon and tape. I already wrote the names on tags and taped them to the gifts." As they went to the car, she explained how Holly could reuse the tags by taping them on the outside of the wrapped gifts. "I thought maybe you could wrap them tonight before you go to bed."

"Then where do I put them? There's not a Christmas tree."

"You can ask Aunt Lydia in the morning." Rachel took the bag of wrapping things from the car, handing it to Holly. Then she got the box herself.

"Will you be here in the morning too?"

"I'll check with Aunt Lydia about that. Okay?"

Holly looked uncertain.

"But I will be here sometime tomorrow. I promise."

Holly was silent as they carried the things to Sarah's bedroom, setting them on the dresser. "There," Rachel said. "You're all set."

"I don't want you to go."

"I can stay until dinner," Rachel offered. "Since it's your birthday."

"No. I mean I don't want you to go home. To Chicago. Not without me."

Rachel hugged her. "I don't want that either, Holly, but there's nothing I can do about it."

"Please, stay here," Holly begged. "Stay with me always."

"I can't stay here. This isn't my home."

"Stay in town, then. You can live at the hotel and come out and see me every day, like you were doing."

"Oh, Holly." Rachel hugged her more tightly. Then to distract her, and perhaps because she wanted to see Benjamin, she suggested they go over and check on Buttercup and Cocoa. Holly eagerly agreed.

"How's the birthday girl?" Benjamin asked when he found them petting Cocoa.

"I get to wrap Christmas presents tonight," Holly told him. "Aunt Rachel shopped them for me, but I get to give them to everyone on Christmas."

"And you've got the hard work of wrapping them," Rachel reminded her.

"The problem is I don't know where to put them after I wrap them," Holly told him. "Aunt Lydia doesn't have a Christmas tree."

He frowned. "That is a problem, isn't it?"

Holly nodded.

"Well, I know where we can get a Christmas tree," he said.

Holly's eyes grew wide. "Can we?"

"I don't know why we can't."

"But Aunt Lydia said no trees in the house," Holly said grimly.

151

"Hmm . . . ?" He glanced around the barn. "Well, this isn't a house."

Holly nodded. "No. It's not."

So it was that the three of them went and chopped down an evergreen tree near the creek and Benjamin secured it to a couple pieces of wood and set it up in the barn. "How's that?" he said when they were finished.

"Beautiful," Holly told him. "Can I decorate it?"

"With what?" Rachel asked.

"My birthday decorations," she told her with twinkling eyes. "Remember?"

Rachel looked at her watch. "It's nearly suppertime. You might have to wait until afterward." She glanced at Benjamin. "Is that okay?"

"It's better than okay." He grinned. "I'll help."

Holly seemed greatly encouraged by their secret Christmas tree, and after dinner, she and Rachel sneaked the birthday decorations from Sarah's bedroom to the barn next door, and Rachel watched as Holly and Benjamin went to work decorating the tree.

"Will we get in trouble?" Holly asked Benjamin as he placed a homemade tinfoil star on top.

He laughed. "I'm Lydia's big brother. Do you think she can boss me around?"

Holly giggled and shook her head.

Watching these two interacting was very reassuring. Rachel felt consoled to know that Benjamin would be so near to Holly after she returned to Chicago tomorrow. She had decided, based on the forecast of a new storm front coming, that she would have to leave by midday tomorrow.

While Holly was paying her regards to Buttercup and Cocoa, Rachel thanked Benjamin for his help. "Having you nearby will make Holly's transition easier," she said. "She needs to know that someone here understands her."

He nodded. "I do understand."

"And if she ever needs to reach me"—Rachel nodded to the phone on the wall—"I'm sure you will be in contact."

"I plan on remaining in contact." His eyes twinkled. "If you don't mind."

She felt her cheeks warming. "I don't mind at all."

He gazed fondly into her eyes and that unexpected rush swept over her again. By now Holly was coming back from greeting the cow and her calf, and Rachel knew Lydia would be wondering where they'd gone. "We'd better get you home," she told Holly. "Especially if you're going to get those packages wrapped tonight."

"I'll walk you girls back," Benjamin told them.

To Rachel's delight, Benjamin suggested they sing Christmas carols as they walk, and all three of them sang with joyful abandon. When they reached the Millers' porch, the door burst open and Lydia frowned suspiciously at them. "Where have you been?" she demanded. "We were worried."

"Out caroling," Benjamin said lightheartedly.

"Caroling?" She shook her head. "It is late. Holly needs to be inside."

"My apologies," Rachel told her. Then she hugged Holly and kissed her good night. "I'll see you in the morning. You better get up to your room now."

Holly gave her a knowing nod. "See you tomorrow, Aunt Rachel."

Lydia remained on the porch after Holly went inside. "We will have a special Christmas breakfast," she told Rachel. "If you would like to come."

"Thank you." Rachel smiled. "I would."

"Then I am sure you will want to be on your way," Lydia said. "Daniel tells me there is snow coming. Maybe by tomorrow night."

"Yes. I heard that too." Rachel told her good night, and Lydia returned into the house, but Benjamin was still there.

"How about a ride home?" he asked as he walked her to the car.

"Seriously?"

His grin glowed in the lantern light. "Sure. I've never been in a car like this."

"Hop in."

"All right!" He blew out the lantern and got into the passenger side. "Cozy, but nice," he told her as she got into the driver's seat. "How about taking me for a little spin around the neighborhood?"

They made pleasant small talk as she drove around a bit. Mostly she talked about Holly, wanting him to know as much as possible about his niece before she had to go. Somehow she felt he was Holly's lifeline. "I feel so much better knowing you'll keep an eye on her," she said as she pulled past the Miller house, where the downstairs windows had already gone dark.

"So you're really leaving tomorrow?" he asked as she pulled into the driveway leading to the Schrock farm.

"It seems like that's best."

"I feel like I've barely gotten to know you, Rachel." He turned to look at her.

"I know." She looked at his face, dimly lit by the dashboard lights. "Me too."

They sat there in silence, and as much as she didn't want him to leave, she couldn't think of a single intelligent thing to say.

"Well, it's been a long day," she said finally, instantly wishing she hadn't.

"*Ja*. And tomorrow will be even longer." He opened the door. "Thanks for the ride, Rachel. See you in the morning."

As she drove back to the hotel, she thought about Benjamin. Was it possible that he had feelings for her? She knew she had feelings for him. The problem was she wasn't absolutely sure about the root of those feelings. What if her attraction to him was simply another part of her desperate desire to hold on to Holly? What if she subconsciously viewed Benjamin as her Amish ticket to fulfilling her selfish need to keep her niece?

14

Holly raced out to meet Rachel even before the car engine stopped. "Merry Christmas!" she cried as Rachel got out of the car.

"Merry Christmas to you too." Now Rachel noticed the bag in Holly's hand. It appeared to be filled with some rustically wrapped gifts. "Where are you taking those?"

"To put under the tree at Uncle Benjamin's."

"Oh?"

"Is that okay?" Holly stood in front of the passenger's side. "Can you drive us there now? I need to hurry."

As they drove the short distance next door, Holly explained her ingenious plan to invite everyone to the barn for a "surprise," where she would show them the tree and present them with their gifts. As she parked by the barn, Rachel hoped that the others would be willing to traipse over here. Before they could get out of the car, Holly glimpsed the presents in the backseat, the ones they'd brought from Chicago. "When are we going to open those, Aunt Rachel?"

"Oh, Holly." Rachel sighed. "I don't think we can do that now."

"Why not?" Holly demanded. "They're from Mommy and Daddy. You said we could open them on Christmas."

"Well, I suppose we could open them, but you know that you won't be able to keep anything that's in those packages. They won't be allowed in Aunt Lydia's house. You know that by now, don't you?"

Holly slumped down into the seat, so low that the big brown bag in her lap seemed to grow bigger. "Yeah . . . I know."

"So maybe we can give those things to some children who don't have any toys," Rachel suggested.

"I don't have any toys," Holly glumly pointed out.

Rachel couldn't help but chuckle at the irony. "Yes, darling, but you have a farm with animals and a cat and a dog and cousins and horses and all sorts of fun things—things that are better than toys. Don't you think?"

"I guess so." Her voice sounded flat.

"So wouldn't you like to share those presents with kids who can really use and enjoy them?"

"I guess so."

"Good. Now I thought you wanted to put those gifts under the Christmas tree. I wonder if it still looks as pretty as it did last night." Rachel got out of the car, hoping her distraction technique would work. She regretted that Holly had spied those gifts. She'd meant to take them back to Chicago without this fuss.

"I thought I recognized that car," Benjamin teased as he walked over.

"I'm putting presents under the tree," Holly cheerfully announced.

"Here you go." He opened the door to the barn for her.

To Rachel's surprise, he wasn't wearing his usual Amish

clothes today. Instead, he had on simple gray cords and a navy polo sweater. "Merry Christmas," she told him as she went inside the barn.

"Uncle Benjamin!" Holly exclaimed. "You have on *normal* clothes today."

He grinned. "You're right. I do. Is that okay with you?"

She nodded with an uneasy expression. "Will you get in trouble?"

Now he laughed. "On Christmas? I sure hope not."

"Can I wear my Christmas dress today?" Holly asked Rachel. "The green velvet one that Mommy got me?"

"Oh . . . I don't think Aunt Lydia would like that too much," Rachel said carefully. "But you look very pretty just as you are, Holly."

"You'd better hurry and get these presents under the tree so we can get over to Aunt Lydia's," Benjamin added. "Mammi is already on her way over and we don't want to be late."

After Holly got the gifts arranged just so, she suggested they should walk back too. "That way we can do more caroling," she told them.

By the time they got to the Miller house, everyone was already seated at the breakfast table, and although Rachel and Benjamin apologized for being late, Lydia gave them a grim look as they took their places. The silent blessing seemed longer than usual, but Rachel suspected this was because of Christmas. However, when it was time to eat, she sensed a stiffness that she suspected was related to her presence. Perhaps she'd been selfish to have come, and yet Holly was so happy to have her here. Plus, she reminded herself, in a few hours she would be out of Lydia's life for good.

After breakfast, Holly insisted on everyone walking over to the barn. At first there was some resistance, but when she told them there were gifts involved, the kids became much more enthused. As expected, Lydia was displeased when she saw their makeshift Christmas tree, but as Holly pointed out, it was "not in the house."

"It's like the telephone," Benjamin teased. "Perfectly at home in the barn."

Holly hand-delivered the gifts to her new family, and the boys seemed pleased as they opened the pocketknife tools that the man at the hardware store had assured Rachel would be useful for young Amishmen. Daniel thanked Holly for the leather-bound blank journal, saying he would use it to keep agricultural records of the weather and crop yield. Sarah was thrilled with a complete set of *Little House on the Prairie* books and promised to read them all to Holly. Lydia even seemed to appreciate the set of pot holders and kitchen towels—and Rachel knew she could use them. Even Holly's grandmother seemed to like the apple-cider-scented candle, and Benjamin grinned when he opened up his brass compass. "Now I'll never get lost," he told Holly, winking at Rachel.

Everyone thanked Holly and then they all trekked back to the house to open the other presents. Rachel tried to stay out of the way, determined to stick around long enough to satisfy Holly, but not long enough to completely ruin Lydia's Christmas. Holly tried to appear thankful when she opened a package containing a faceless rag doll, but Rachel could tell she was disappointed. It would not make up for losing her beloved Bunny or Ivy. It didn't take long until the gifting ended and everyone was in a merry mood, showing others their treasures and chattering happily together. Meanwhile Rachel lurked in the shadows, biding her time.

Holly was sitting on Daniel's lap again. They were looking at a bird book someone had given him. Suddenly the two were tickling and teasing. Holly reached up and tugged playfully on his beard. He let out an exaggerated "yee-ouch!" which made Holly break into hysterical giggles. The game went into full gear as she tugged and he pretended to be in pain.

Unfortunately, Lydia was glowering as she watched this friendly scene unfolding. "Holly," she finally said in a stern tone. "Stop doing that *at once!*" The room got quiet, and everyone seemed to be staring at Holly. "And get down from there," Lydia told her. "Mind your manners, child."

Holly got down, but she was glaring at Lydia, and Rachel could tell by her eyes she was about to blow up. "I don't *have* to mind you," Holly said defiantly. "You're *not* my mommy. You're not even my aunt Rachel. You're just a big mean old *witch!*"

"Holly!" Rachel exclaimed in horror.

"Go to your room!" Lydia barked at Holly. "Do not come down until you can repent and ask forgiveness." Then Lydia turned away and marched off toward the kitchen.

Rachel was dumbstruck, but she took Holly by the hand and solemnly led her upstairs. Once they were behind closed doors, she asked Holly why she'd done that. "Because she is mean," Holly said in a trembling voice. "I don't like her."

"But you know better than to talk like that—to anyone."

"I know." Holly sighed. "It just came out of me."

"You'll have to say you're sorry."

"I'm *not* sorry."

"Well, stay up here and think about it, Holly. Maybe you'll start to feel sorry."

"Where are you going?"

"To talk to Aunt Lydia . . . to see if I can help smooth this over." She almost added "before I go home," but she didn't want to send Holly over another emotional ledge.

Rachel looked around the house, which had settled back into a subdued sense of festiveness, but Lydia seemed to have disappeared.

"She's probably in the barn," Benjamin whispered in Rachel's ear. So Rachel went out through the kitchen and across to the barn, and discovered he was right. Lydia was stewing out in the same stall where Buttercup had struggled to give birth not long ago.

"Holly will apologize to you," Rachel told Lydia as she approached the stony-looking figure. With her arms folded tightly around her middle and feet planted apart, Lydia reminded Rachel of how Holly acted when she wanted her way.

"I *know* she will." Lydia turned her back to Rachel, facing the wall. "You do not need to tell me that."

"It's just that she needs some time."

"I know that too," she snapped.

"She's been through a lot." Rachel wasn't ready to give up. "And she's got a lot of adjusting to do. I just hope you can be patient with her."

Lydia whirled around. "I am a very patient woman."

Rachel tried not to look too skeptical, but she held her tongue.

"This is not easy for me. Holly is a very stubborn child."

"Holly is perfectly normal—for a seven-year-old who's been through a lot."

"She is *spoiled*—just like her mother was spoiled."

Rachel took in a sharp breath. "Please, do not speak like that about Miri."

"Miriam was *my* sister. I will speak as I like about her. She was spoiled and Holly is spoiled. They are two of a kind."

"How can you be so hateful—not only to a little girl, but to someone who is dead?" Rachel asked.

"Hateful?" Lydia looked stunned. "I *loved* Miriam. But she hurt me deeply. I never thought she would leave us like she—"

"Really?" It was Benjamin's voice. "Sorry to intrude, but I followed Rachel out here, and now I want to put in my two cents." He came over to stand by Rachel in front of the stall. "After all, Miriam was my sister and Holly is my niece. Shouldn't I have a voice in this too, Lydia?"

Lydia glowered at him. "You? Look at yourself, Benjamin Schrock! You do not even know how to dress proper. Why should I listen to you?"

"Because I know what's troubling you, Lydia." His voice grew gentler now. "I know how you blame yourself that Miriam left like she did. Maybe you even blame yourself for her death."

Lydia's brow creased and she tightened her folded arms around her middle, as if trying to pull into herself.

"You see, Daniel was in love with Miriam," he explained to Rachel. "It was a long time ago and some people may have forgotten, but everyone in this family knew about it."

"*Ja*, that is true. Daniel did love Miriam, but Miriam did not love Daniel." Lydia held her chin up.

"That's right." Benjamin nodded. "But Miriam was willing to marry Daniel," he told Rachel. "When Daed pressured her, Miriam was about to cave." He turned to Lydia. "But *who* discouraged her to marry? *Who* encouraged her to leave the settlement? *Who* gave her some money to get her started out in the English world?"

Lydia said nothing, but it was clear that she didn't like hearing those words.

Benjamin moved close to Lydia now, putting an arm around her shoulders. "And I don't hold it against you, Lydia. I think it was the kindest thing you could've done for our sister. We both know she never would've been happy here. She didn't fit in. She didn't want to. You gave her the wings to fly."

Lydia's stony countenance crumbled and she fell sobbing onto Benjamin's shoulder. "But now she is gone—and it is my fault she can never come back. It is my fault, Benjamin. I made her leave. I did. I did."

Rachel went over and put an arm around Lydia. "It's no more your fault than it is mine, Lydia. And sometimes I blame myself for both their deaths—my brother and your sister."

Lydia looked at her with moist eyes. "You do?"

She nodded. "When Michael told me his plans to take Miri to the Caribbean for their anniversary, I thought it was a bad idea. I had this strong innate sense that they shouldn't go. But I said nothing. Instead I offered to stay with Holly. And then they both died. Do you know how that makes me feel?"

"Guilty?"

Rachel nodded. "But Miri and Michael were adults. They made their own choices, and like Benjamin said, Miri would never have been happy here. You gave her the freedom to leave, Lydia. She lived a very fulfilled life. She loved her husband and she loved Holly."

"Did she love God?" Lydia's brow creased in worry.

"I believe she did," Rachel assured her. "We talked about faith sometimes. She went to church occasionally. People live out their beliefs in different ways, but I'm convinced that both my brother and your sister are with God now."

Lydia looked relieved.

"So you have to stop blaming yourself for Miriam," Benjamin told Lydia. "It's not good for you and it is hurting Holly." He tilted his head to one side. "Why were you so hard on Holly today? She was just playing, but you came down hard on her, Lydia. Why was that?"

There was a long silence. Rachel was glad he'd asked this question and was curious as to Lydia's answer.

"It wasn't like Holly did anything the other children haven't done," Benjamin pressed. "Why did you react like that?"

She closed her eyes and shook her head. "Seeing Holly like that, being so strong willed and rebellious," Lydia said quietly, "brought Miriam back . . . and it scared me."

"Why did it scare you?" Benjamin asked.

"I saw how Daniel was playing with Holly. I knew in my heart that he was remembering Miriam. I could see it in his eyes. It felt like Miriam was taking him away from me again. This time through Holly. I became jealous again—like I was jealous of Miriam those years ago."

Rachel and Benjamin exchanged worried glances.

"That's not good," Benjamin said solemnly.

"I *know* that." She grimaced. "Jealousy is sinful and selfish and vain. I do not *want* to feel that way. I do not. I promise I will repent."

"But it's not fair to Holly," Benjamin told her. "She's the one who will suffer for your selfishness, Lydia."

"I know," Lydia muttered.

"Lydia." His tone grew very firm. "You know in your heart that Holly belongs with Rachel. Don't you?"

She looked down at the floor, saying nothing.

"Remember the Bible story about the rich, powerful man who had lots of sheep, but he insisted on taking the other man's one and only lamb? Remember how that was a wrong that needed to be righted?" Benjamin asked.

She nodded reluctantly. "I remember that story."

"You have four wonderful children, Lydia. You have nieces and nephews. Your mother lives right next door, and you will have grandchildren before long. I know Jacob has his eye on the Fisher girl."

"*Ja*. Anna is a good girl for Jacob." She nodded as if imagining grandchildren.

"God has blessed you abundantly, Lydia."

"*Ja*. That is true."

"Do you *hear* what I'm saying to you?" Benjamin asked her. "Do you know what I mean?"

She let out a long sigh. "Holly belongs to Rachel. I know this is true."

Rachel's heart gave a little leap. "Do you really mean that?" she asked Lydia. "You truly believe that Holly belongs with me?"

"*Ja*," Lydia said with a sigh. "She loves you so much. That will never change. She can remain with you . . . she can go home with you."

Rachel hugged Lydia tightly. "Thank you! Thank you! *Thank you!*"

"*Ja*." Lydia smiled meekly. "Merry Christmas to you!"

"Merry Christmas to you too!" Rachel felt like dancing. "And you'll still be her aunt, and it would be wonderful if Holly could visit you sometimes. I mean, if that's okay with you."

"I would like that." Lydia's face warmed with a smile. "Very much. And you can come too, Rachel."

"Thank you." Rachel turned to Benjamin, beaming at him with gratitude. "And Holly could come visit you too."

"You mean *if* I'm still here."

Lydia looked surprised. "You are leaving? *What?*"

He shrugged. "Eventually I will leave. It was always my plan. And you know that your boys are nearly ready to take over Mamm's farm."

"But where will you go?" Lydia looked dismayed.

Benjamin peered longingly at Rachel. "I don't know for sure," he said slowly. "Maybe Chicago for a while."

"Chicago?" Lydia looked from Benjamin to Rachel and then, like the dawning sun, realization washed over her face. "You mean to see *Rachel*? And to see Holly?"

"If they're willing to get to know me better." He gave Rachel a hopeful look.

Rachel reached for his hand now, squeezing it in her own. "You *know* we are, Benjamin."

He smiled shyly but didn't release Rachel's fingers. "Who knows . . . in time I might be able to convince them to move closer to family," he told Lydia. "Somewhere around here perhaps."

"Rachel and Holly would move to be near *us*?" Lydia's brow creased as she studied Rachel. "Would you truly do that, Rachel?"

"I don't think either of us would miss the big city too much," Rachel confessed to her.

"Because we all need family," Benjamin said. "Not just at Christmastime either." He squeezed her hand warmly.

Lydia nodded. "*Ja.* That's true. Now I will go and tell Holly this news." She paused then, looking uncertainly at Rachel. "Or do you want to tell her?"

"No, it's okay. You go tell her." Rachel smiled.

After Lydia left, Benjamin was still holding Rachel's hand and he turned to look into her eyes. "I hope I didn't overstep any boundaries just now," he said apologetically.

"Not where I'm concerned." She smiled up at him.

"Because I don't want to lose you," he said gently. "Even if that means I have to live in Chicago for a while."

She reached for his other hand now. "You're not going to lose me, Benjamin. Whether or not you move to Chicago."

They stood just gazing at each other for a long moment and then he leaned down, tenderly kissing her. "Merry Christmas," he said quietly.

"Merry Christmas." She felt nearly dizzy with joy now. "This is turning out to be the best Christmas ever."

"For me too," he said happily. "And I predict that from this day forward, you will always spend Christmas surrounded by loved ones and family, Rachel."

"Should we go see how Holly has received this news?"

He nodded as he wrapped an arm around her, holding her close as the two of them walked back to the house. Then just as they neared the front porch, white fluffy snowflakes began to tumble joyfully down from the sky.

Melody Carlson is the award-winning author of over two hundred books, including *Christmas at Harrington's*, *The Christmas Shoppe*, and *The Christmas Pony*. Melody recently received a Romantic Times Career Achievement Award in the inspirational market for her books. She and her husband live in central Oregon. For more information about Melody, visit her website at www.melodycarlson.com.

Meet Melody at
MelodyCarlson.com

- Enter a contest for a signed book
- Read her monthly newsletter
- Find a special page for book clubs
- Discover more books by Melody

Become a fan on Facebook

Melody Carlson Books

Sometimes the best gift is a second chance.

You will love Melody Carlson's bestselling *Christmas at Harrington's*, a story full of redemption and true holiday spirit.

With Christmas around the corner, the Turnbull family is in need of a few small miracles.

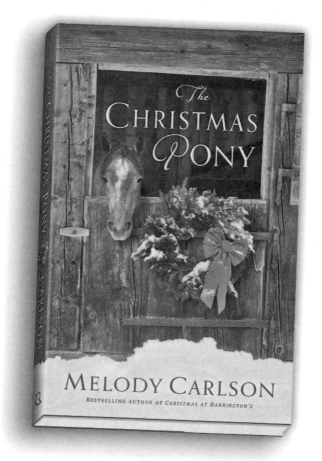

It is 1937, and Lucy Turnbull knows better than to wish for a pony this Christmas. Her mother has assured her in no uncertain terms that asking for a pony is the same as asking for the moon. Then an interesting pair of strangers comes to town, and Lucy's world changes forever.

The small town of PARRISH SPRINGS is not quite ready for MATILDA HONEYCUTT.

When a strange visitor opens a very unusual Christmas shop on Main Street, the residents of a small town discover that *sometimes miracles are found where you least expect them.*

"Fisher writes with her heart and soul."

—*Romantic Times*

When a young couple is stranded at an Amish farm over Christmas, both families are in for a new experience—and a chance to heal old wounds.

Revell

a division of Baker Publishing Group
www.RevellBooks.com

Available Wherever Books Are Sold
Also Available in Ebook Format

DON'T MISS THE
LANCASTER COUNTY *Secrets* SERIES!

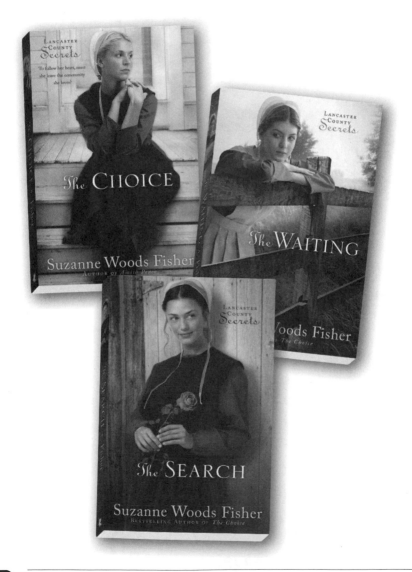